The Flatland Chronicles

The Flatland Chronicles

Ken White

White & Wilkinson

Photograph by Linda Scheller.

THE FLATLAND CHRONICLES

KEN WHITE
1108 WELLESLEY AVENUE
MODESTO, CA 95350-5044
209-567-0600
KENWHITE@KW209.COM

Published in the United States of America
ISBN: 978-1-7340222-9-2 (Soft Cover)
ISBN: 978-1-7340222-0-5 (Case Bound)
ISBN: 978-1-7354384-1-2 (ebook)

1. Fiction / General
2. Fiction / Regional

Library of Congress Control Number: 2020916257

Summary: *The Flatland Chronicles* is a fictional memoir in the style of the *Spoon River Anthology* by Edgar Lee Masters. Instead of poems, it is a collection of short, short stories about life in California's Central Valley.

2430 Tully Road, Suite 20-058 | Modesto, California 95350 USA 1.209.567.0600 |
www.whitewilkinsonpub.com

Dedication

To Jack Leach, who taught me a love of the written word. And to the other Flatlanders who love the Valley as deeply as the leaf loves the bough.

Special Thanks

Robin. My family. Ron Wilkinson. Carl Baggese. Chris Murphy/*ModestoView*. And to all those writers who are dedicated to telling the stories of the Central Valley.

Acknowledgements

Wendell White, George Rogers, Stephan Marlow, John Reed, Rod Patterson, Paul Leinberger, Alan Arnopole, Genevieve Beltran, Susan Crosby, Linda Peterson, The Ratz - Pat Durr, Danny Johnson, Rick Edmond, and Ray Rector, *Penumbra* Magazine, *Spectrum* Magazine, and Ray Bradbury.

Introduction

"Language is a country, and the heart is a country, and at their shared borders we encounter the geography of home."
– *Christopher Buckley and Gary Young, "The Geography of Home"*

California has long been the source of inspiration for writers. The landscape and people, the expectations and possibilities, the history and diversity have all influenced those who call this place home.

I was born and raised in the Central Valley Heartland of California. This place and its people have shaped who I am and how I look at the world. That is what I explore in *The Flatland Chronicles*, a fictional memoir in the style of the *Spoon River Anthology* by Edgar Lee Masters. Instead of poems, I write short, short stories about life in the Central Valley.

Although I explore the Central Valley experience, my work celebrates the human condition: our hopes, dreams, joys, fears, and concerns as individuals and a people. It explores our common humanity. What it is to be a Californian, an American, and a human.

Ken White
Modesto, California
Winter 2021

Prologue

"The older I get, the more clearly I remember things that never happened."
– *Mark Twain*

The Great Central Valley. This is what I know. My name is KW. Around here, they call me The Flatlander. Here is Modesto, California. The town where summer lasts longer. It's a small town. Least it was when I was growing up. I was born here, raised here, will die here. Way out in Summer Country. I like summer. I wish it could last forever.

Acclaimed author Joan Didion, a Central Valley patriot and refugee, once wrote that "a place belongs forever to whoever claims it hardest, remembers it most obsessively, wrenches it from itself, shapes it, renders it, loves it so radically that he remakes it in his own image." I believe that. My hometown belongs to me. The Valley is mine.

It is my touchstone and tap root, not a flat spot on the map glanced in the rearview on the way to someplace else. From it I draw sustenance, inspiration, and determination. The stories I tell take place here and involve those who live here. They are tales conjured by a place, people, and events – real, imagined, and/or recollected. They have all shaped who I am and how I see the world. It's the truth, it's actual. Everything is matter-of-factual.

This is my personal remembrance of things past, present, and future. The five senses conjuring déjà vu and the familiar as surely as Proust's tea-dipped *madeleines*. This is my chronicle of what I believe. That in my world – change is inevitable, expectations unreal, loneliness absolute, and laughter essential.

In Ray Bradbury's coming-of-age novel, *Dandelion Wine*, 12-year-old Douglas Spaulding and his younger brother, Tom, write down all the things they experienced during the summer of 1928 as they experienced them. It is a list of all the stories they could tell. Things like how many baseball games they played, how many times they washed their hands or brushed their teeth, hours they slept, apples and pears they ate, books they read, matinees they saw, how many lollipops, Tootsie Rolls, and ice cream cones they had.

In their yellow nickel tablet, they chronicled with a Ticonderoga pencil the summer statistics; the things they did over-and-over again each darn summer, which they labeled "Rites and Ceremonies." Like making dandelion wine, buying new tennis shoes, shooting off the first firecracker, making lemonade, getting slivers in their feet, picking wild fox grapes, their first root beer pop, first time running barefoot in the grass, first time almost drowning in the lake, first watermelon, first mosquito, and first harvest of dandelions.

Then there were the things they did for the first time ever, which they put under "Discoveries and Revelations." Like eating olives, finding out that maybe their grandpa or dad didn't know everything in the world, that they were alive, that night is the result of shadows crawling out from under five billion trees, and that every time you bottled dandelion wine you got a whole chunk of 1928 put away safe.

The following is my list. These are the stories I have to tell.

These stories are my time machine. As you read them, I hope you are transported to your own once upon a time and happily ever after.

Collectively, they are *The Flatland Chronicles*.

Act I. Youth/6AM – Noon
It's just before dawn. A brand-new day. Everything is fresh and new. I can see yesterday from here.

Act II. Middle Age/Noon – 6PM
It's mid-day. I am surrounded by the here-and-now. Time to slow down a bit and gather energy for the final push.

Act III. Old Age/6PM – Midnight
It's sunset. The day is just about done. Time to reflect on what will, may, or can be.

Epilogue. Midnight – 6AM
It's midnight in Modesto. Time to dream. What will be, will be. See you next time around. Carry on.

"Then I reflected that all things happen, happen to one, precisely now. Century follows century, and things happen only in the present. There are countless men in the air, on land and at sea, and all that really happens happens to me."
– *Jorge Luis Borges, Ficciones*

"Ever-Present Past"

There are places I'll remember
All my life, though some have changed
Some forever, not for better
Some have gone and some remain
All these places have their moments
With lovers and friends I still can recall
Some are dead and some are living
In my life, I've loved them all.
– Lennon and McCartney, "In My Life."

In the legend of Oedipus, the Sphinx posed a riddle to all who tried to pass the road she guarded. If they failed, they died. She asked, "What walks on four feet in the morning, on two at noon, and on three in the evening?" Oedipus solved the riddle by replying, "Man crawls on all fours as a baby, walks upright in the prime of life, and uses a staff in old age." The Sphinx then killed herself.

Like the riddle's three ages of man, our lives are a trilogy, a triad, a triptych. Yesterday, Today, and Tomorrow. Act I, Act II, and Act III. Separation, Initiation, and Return. Home, Away, and Back Home Again. Morning, Noon, and Night. Here, There, and Everywhere. Past and future coexist in a continuum of now.

At each stage of life, we journey down roads that are familiar and well-traveled, having driven them our entire life. They are the roads taken. The landmarks we pass are beloved and well-known.

Although many of these roads are the same ones we've been down before, they are different. We are different. We may pass someone along the way who looks familiar, only to realize that it was, is, or will be us in an earlier, current, or imagined incarnation. Like Albert Finney and Audrey Hepburn in *Two for the Road*.

January is the coldest month of the year. Named after Janus, the Roman god of doorways, it is the month of new beginnings, comebacks, and second chances. Janus is the god of doors, transitions, gates, and change. A two-faced god, he looks at what was and will be. Janus is the master of time because he can see into the past with one face and into the future with the other. As the god of beginnings, he represents the harvest, marriages, and deaths, as well as the limbo between barbarism and civilization, rural and urban, youth and adulthood.

Not unlike Janus, I am forever suspended between two worlds, two realities. Standing here in the now contemplating the road behind and the road ahead. Trapped in the moment, one face looking backward, one face looking forward. I have seen the past, suffered these events in the present, and foretold the future. I am reminded of Neil Young caught in the act on the cover of *Buffalo Springfield Again*, staring at what's gone before while the rest of the band gaze at what could be.

Each New Year's Eve, as I stand in the doorway listening to *Auld Lang Syne*, I am reminded of the ever-present past.

The Greek philosopher Heraclitus wrote, "No man ever steps in the same river twice, for it's not the same river and he's not the same man." It's true. I can look upriver and recall where and who I was, look at where I'm standing knee-deep in the current and see where and who I am now, then look down river and imagine where or who I will be. It is all connected. It is all one endless, flowing stream.

And the seasons they go 'round and 'round
And the painted ponies go up and down
We're captive on the carousel of time
We can't return, we can only look behind
From where we came
And go round and 'round and 'round
In the circle game

And go 'round and 'round and 'round in the circle game.
– Joni Mitchell, "The Circle Game"

Each and every day, I encounter people and places, sights and sounds, memories and mementos that are, or symbolize, my ever-present past – the then, now, and yet-to-be of my life. It is a chronicle of the immediate past, present, and future.

Yesterday when I was young, I spoke, understood, and thought as a child. As a middle-aged man, I put away those childish things. As a senior citizen, I will long for those young boy days and ways.

I left home to grow up. I journeyed the country and the world to grow wise. I came back to grow old.

Once I enjoyed being together, then I enjoyed being alone; now I enjoy being together again.

I used to hate girls, then I puppy-loved young ladies, and now I adore women.

As a child, I feared rejection, now I fear change, and someday, I will fear the unknown.

Back in the day, I needed to win, now I just want to play, and down the road I just want to show up.

Once upon a time, I wrote book reports. Now I write fiction. Tomorrow I will write remembrances.

At Del Webb Field, I played a Little League championship back then, now I play softball at Davis Park with some old kids, and someday I will play catch at Pike Park with my grandchildren.

I used to listen to rock, now it's new age, next it will be the golden oldies.

I drove a '52 Chevy, now I drive a Honda, next I'll drive a walker.

I grew up watching Howdy Doody, now it's anything on PBS, someday it will be reruns of *thirtysomething*.

I used to drink RC Cola, now it's beer, next it will be Metamucil.

I sat in the dark watching *Darby O'Gill and the Little People*, now it's indy films at the State Theatre, and in the future, it will be *It's a Wonderful Life* in Immerse-O-Vision.

My hero was Mickey Mantle. Today it's my wife, family, friends, and community. Someday it will be my doctor.

As a child, my favorite teacher was Jack Leach, today it's Joseph Campbell, tomorrow it will be Andrew Weil.

I dreamed of going to Disneyland, now it's Machu Picchu, tomorrow it will be anywhere.

My legacy was my enthusiasm, now it's building community, while tomorrow it will be spreading the word.

I ruptured my spleen playing baseball at Pike Park, I tore my ACL playing flag football at Thousand Oaks Park, and someday I'll throw my arm out playing horseshoes at Enslen Park.

The McHenry Mansion was a boarding house, now it's a museum, tomorrow it will be an empty lot.

I once was a student at Garrison, now it's MJC4Life, and then it will be DailyOM.

Ninth Street was old Highway 99 with gas stations and car dealerships, now it's a commercial throughway, and tomorrow it will be abandoned buildings.

Yesterday I worked at Bi-Rite Market, today I work for myself, and tomorrow I will work for the future.

My mornings were once filled with playing grab-ass, my noons are now filled with doing good, and my evenings will soon be filled with memories.

The Arch was, is, and will be.

I look forward to the next cycle of the circle.

"I was born, raised and lowered in Modesto, California, USA."
– George Rogers, Poet and Friend

"Fog Holiday"

City Hospital was empty. All the family and friends had left their loved ones to face the night alone. I was sitting in the second floor sunroom counting the seconds between the signal light changes at the corner of 17th and H Streets. The rain drizzles on the windowpane gave the colored lights a surreal, aqueous glow. Twelve years old, alone in a hospital. Bleak, very bleak.

I still dream about those dark nights.

I touched the bandage around my stomach. It felt like it was holding in my guts. It was. Everything but the spleen the surgeons had removed. The spleen that had ruptured when Ernie had jumped to avoid the tag at second and kneed me in the stomach. The spleen the doctors said I didn't need because it was a vestigial organ, whatever that meant. It sounded like "vestal virgins," which I had read about in Roman mythology, but I knew it wasn't the same. It was the same body part that kills jet pilots who parachute out of their planes over the ocean, hit the water, rupture their spleens, and bleed to death. The same organ that had just pumped two pints of blood into my stomach cavity. Enough blood that if Mom hadn't taken me to the doctor right away and the doctor hadn't recognized the symptoms right away and hadn't carried me out to the car in his arms right away, I could have died. I would find out later how really close to death I was.

In 1962, my family lived at 1500 Del Vista, adjacent to Pike Park, which was our home away from home all year long. Our very own oasis with a swing set, sand box, baseball diamond, and wide-open fields. During the summer, we'd be there from sunrise to sunset. We played baseball no matter what season it was.

Except now, as February counted down. I was still recovering from the splenectomy. And it was killing me. No baseball, no running, no nothing. No matter what. The weather got worse after my get-well party. When it wasn't foggy, it was too cold. When it wasn't too cold, it was raining. The streets were flooded. I burrowed inside and couldn't wait until I was better, and the days were longer. Spring Training was just around the corner. So were the tryouts for the Babe Ruth League, which was the next step in local organized baseball after Little League. It had been three weeks since the accident and I was getting bored and antsy. I was ready to start playing ball again, now that I'd conveniently forgotten and buried what had put me on the disabled list in the first place.

There had been no school that February day. The tule fog was so thick, it was too dangerous to drive. The city schools canceled classes, and us guys immediately grabbed our baseball mitts, bats, and balls and headed out to Pike Park for a game of lob ball. It was cold and wet and miserable, but we didn't care. We loved baseball. We only had enough guys to play the left side of the infield, so we closed off the right side and made pitcher as good as first. The ball had to be hit to the left of an imaginary line drawn from home plate through the pitcher's mound, across second base, out into center field, and through the Coca-Cola plant across the street. Anything hit to the right of that line was foul. The Coca-Cola plant had a vending machine in the lobby that had the coldest Cokes in town for just ten cents. We always made time for a Coke break on a hot day, if we had gotten, and still had, our allowances.

I was playing short. I was wearing my steel baseball spikes. I'm not sure why. Maybe because I didn't want to slip and hurt myself. Maybe because they made me feel like a big leaguer, like Mickey Mantle, my hero. Ernie was standing on first. He was a year older than us and the neighborhood bully. He lived next to my best friend, Gary. Bobby, another neighborhood kid, was up. He slapped an easy one-hopper to me. A tailor-made, double-play ball. I snagged it and raced to tag second before Ernie got there. We arrived at the bag at the same time. Ernie was barefoot, so he jumped to avoid getting spiked. And planted his knee in my belly.

The next thing I knew, I was on my back. I was white as a ghost, clammy, and kind of sick to my stomach. My buddies helped me up. Roy, another neighbor kid, and my best friend until Gary came along, said I didn't look so good. He grabbed my stuff and walked me and Tim, my younger brother, home.

When we stepped inside the house, Mom froze as soon as she saw me. Roy left and I went into the bathroom. I felt like I had to pee but couldn't. I felt like I had to poop but couldn't. I had a pain in my left shoulder. That was all Doctor Robinson needed to hear when my mother called. He told her to bring me in right away. When we got to his office, he checked me over, asked a few questions, and said I needed to go to the hospital. He picked me up and carried me to the car. I was shocked because he wasn't all that big and seemed kind of old at the time. Plus, if he was doing that, I figured it must be bad. It was.

While I was recovering in my room following the surgery, Dr. Nachtman visited me with a present. My spleen in a glass jar of formaldehyde. It was gross. When my parents arrived, he said a few words to them and left.

"I'm not fuzzy anymore," I proudly told my mother.

"The anesthesia must be wearing off," Dad replied.

It wasn't.

"No," I corrected him, still a little groggy. "I'm not fuzzy down there," I said, pointing below my stomach. The summer before I had started sprouting pubic hair and Mom had mercilessly teased me about it. During prep for the surgery, they had shaved me clean.

For a week after I came home from the hospital, I would crawl into my parents' bed in the middle of the night. It had scared me pretty good, and I couldn't sleep. One night, my father said, "You've got to stop doing this, son."

"But I'm afraid," I said.

"Then tell us a story," Mom said. "You know," she added, "there are cultures all over the world that have men who have looked death in the face and returned to tell stories of enlightenment and healing that helped the tribe survive. They call them shamans. Tell us a story, Michael."

And I did.

Photograph by Helmut Hammersen.

"Bulletproof"

In memory of Dave Threlfall.

We dodged the bullet more times than we could remember. As teen-agers, as young men, as adults. Me and my high school buddy and college roommate, now my brother-in-law. (The Valley can be complicated and incestuous when it comes to family.) We couldn't recall all the stories. Of course, his wife and his sister – now my wife – didn't want their impressionable children to hear those stories.

There had been so many opportunities to bite the bullet. Riding box cars out to Del Rio to fish golf balls out of water hazards. Driving through 4-way stops in the country with the headlights off. Paying a bum to buy us Sloe Gin. Good and bad drugs. Good and bad sex. Vietnam. Driving drunk. Getting into fights. Partying with bikers we'd met at a strip club. Scoring drugs from junkies while waiting in line at Winterland.

We were lucky. Someone was watching out for us. There but fortune and all that, looking back.

The son of an old friend wasn't so fortunate. He was eighteen. Making some serious noise with a local punk band. Something his father had aspired to but never achieved. He was left to die alone in an orchard after overdosing on heroin. He couldn't dodge the bullet.

"He found all the silvers
of the earth's pure form
but the silver found the bullet
and the bullet found him."
– *Stephan Marlow, "Lorca"*

"Ball Dudes"

On the television, Barry Bonds shoots a line drive foul that nearly decapitates old Mike Walt.

Mike is a ball dude, one of two old farts hired by the Giants to patrol the foul lines chasing balls and

tossing them to the fans before the fans fall out of the stands trying to get a souvenir. Kruk and Kuip, the

play-by-play and color guys, point out that Mike and Mike Johnson, the other ball dude, had grown up

together in Escalon, a little town just down the Stanislaus River from Modesto, and had played baseball

together since third grade.

"That'll be us," I tell Gary, who reclines on the couch sucking slowly on a Pediapop. We, too, have

been best friends and teammates since third grade. I played second and wore #7, in honor of Mickey

Mantle, the Mick. He played first and wore #30, in honor of Orlando Cepeda, the Baby Bull.

"Someday," he says, a little out of breath, in between long draws on the medicinal popsicle. "Be a

little tough to bend over with this," he adds, pointing at the stoma that feeds the plastic sack of body waste

dangling at his emaciated waist.

"Hell, old Mike can't touch his toes either," I reply.

Just then, old Mike lets one scoot between his legs, loses his balance, and topples ass-over-

teakettle.

"Maybe," Gary says, and we both chuckle.

As I stand beside the wooden casket floating above the dark hole in the bright September sun, the day after the Giants sweep the Dodgers, I think of the ball dudes and all the other things my best friend and I will never do as planned.

You see, cancer bats last.

"The Hunter"

The 17-year-old boy had never killed anything. His best friend talked him into going rabbit hunting in an uncle's vineyard. The morning of the shoot, he was given a 12-gauge shotgun, some shells, and a few words of caution. Mainly to know where everyone was.

He set off down a row of vines. The sun was high, and he was sweating. When the rabbit hopped into his row and stopped, he was as shocked to see the rabbit as the rabbit was to see him. He put the gun to his shoulder, aimed, clicked off the safety, and fired. When the blue haze and thunder cleared, he saw the rabbit lying there, twitching. Heart thumping, he raced to where it lay. He nudged it with his tennis shoe. It was dead.

That was the last time he ever shot a living thing.

That night, his father, who had joined the Marines as a 17-year-old, told him, "I'll drive you to Canada tomorrow."

Artwork by Jackson Leverone.

"Last Chance Angel"

It was hot and he was late. He paid, got the keys, and slid into the driver's seat, hoping the mechanic hadn't left grease stains on the upholstery.

She shuffled up, all bad teeth and street-beaten obeisance.

Can't they keep these people out of here, he thought.

She wasn't that old. She wore the cuffs rolled up on her worn Levi's and pink flip-flops. Her stringy hair was tied up with a faded bandanna. Her eyes were a little off.

She spoke, but he couldn't hear her through the rolled-up glass. The automatic window wasn't working that day either, so he opened the door a crack.

"'Scuse me, I just need fifty cents," she said. "For some milk."

Right, he thought, *if Gallo made milk*.

"I'm sorry," he said, smiling and waving his hand and wishing she were gone. He wasn't sure why he rejected her request immediately. He almost always gave these people something.

"How 'bout fifteen cents?"

"Sorry."

"Five cents. Anything."

"Sorry," and he closed the door.

She shrugged and stutter-stepped off to ask the young Mexican man who was busy cleaning up behind the garage. She followed him around, hand outstretched. He didn't even look at her. She gave up and disappeared around a corner.

Out of sight, out of mind.

He stowed everything away, happy to be back in the familiar territory of his car. He started to check his cell phone for messages when a shadow darkened the screen.

She was back. She held out her weather-wrinkled hand.

"Fifteen cents," she said. "I got fifteen cents." She smiled and fluttered away toward the convenience store across the street.

He pulled out and headed home.

He was listening to his cell messages and never saw the truck that ran the red light.

"I Never Cried for My Mother"

"Just remember, we're all in this alone."
– *Lily Tomlin*

We sat, sorta-watching "Giants Vision," and trying to talk above the noise at the Brew Pub. I was working through some more guilt and Gary was sounding the board.

It's her birthday. I would have sent a card by now. I would have phoned. By then, she would have had too many glasses of wine, but she would still have been happy to hear from her number one son. We would have made small talk. She would have

repeated herself a number-of-times, told me things she had just told me last week or last minute. Timing was everything with these calls. If I caught her too late, it would not be a good conversation. I would get angry, trying to browbeat her long distance into taking better care of herself. She would get upset and the call would be over. And I could avoid the reality of what was happening for another week.

Then she was dead. And I could make the comment I had just made to Gary; a statement that was true, that I really didn't mean, but had said anyway. "I'm glad I don't have a mother to have to worry about shopping for or sending a card to." I realized that it didn't come out the way it was supposed to.

"That's not how you feel, and you know it," he said.

"I meant I wish she was still here, but I'm glad we didn't make a big deal out of buying gifts."

"But she always expected one."

"And I always sent her a card. I think I was the only one in the whole family who never bought a gift on Father's Day, Mother's Day, or their birthdays. Just one more example of how I wasn't as much a part of the family as I thought. I was just never there for them. Especially at the end."

"Why do you keep beating yourself up? Why should you feel bad? She lived her life the way she wanted. Nobody was going to change that. Not even you."

"She was pretty stubborn."

"And none of us would have ever changed that. She died. You couldn't stop that. You can't stop time. You've got to keep moving. There are a lot more days ahead. So put your energy into making those good instead of worrying about what you didn't do and couldn't help."

For them both – my mom and Sandy – I had become what the therapists call a "coalcoholic": the caretaker, the giver of hope, the ignorer of oppressive reality. I gave them a fix as deadly as their addiction. I satisfied their dependency; their need to be needed. I shot them up with blind faith and unquestioning support.

I wasn't there when she died. Typical. I hadn't spent much time with her or the rest of the family since Sandy and I got married and moved away. We went down for Thanksgiving and Christmas, then once every month or so. It was hard, but it was one of the compromises you make to sustain a marriage. So, I really didn't know what was going on. I blamed it on Sandy, but I realize now it was a defense. If I ignored the problems – my mother's drinking, her health, her behavior – it would go away. It did. About a week after she visited us. I told her she was drinking too much and refused to make her any more drinks. It was easy to be righteous when you didn't have to deal with it every day like Dad and the rest of the family. I remember my sisters telling me stories about Dad passing out because he tried to drink all the booze in the house so she wouldn't have any. It was the only way he could tell her no. He knew she was killing herself, but he just couldn't stop her. It wasn't in him. He loved her too much.

I begin to realize how much like him I really am. Easier to give in and ignore it than confront it.

And that's why I really stayed away. When I just talked to them over the phone, I didn't have to see what was going on and didn't have to admit it. So, I wasn't there when her heart stopped. I wasn't there sitting in the dining room with the rest of the family while she lay on the couch, waiting for the ambulance to take her away. I arrived later, after she was already gone. I had avoided it again. And I probably would have ducked out of the next few days of mourning if I could have.

I never cried for her. Gary did. The night of the wake. I heard him. And I, the practical, no-nonsense, always-in-control eldest son, thought he'd had too much beer and was just throwing up. He wasn't.

It wasn't until months later that I began to deal with some of the guilt and hurt. I did, as we usually do, in dreams. I was in the living room, sitting on the coffee table by the couch; the old, broken-down couch with the maple coffee and end-tables. At her feet was the black and white television. On one end-table was her Kleenex, her plastic glass of water, and all her medicine. It was here that she went each night to pass out. After she'd doused the emptiness with alcohol. I guess it might have been the night she died. She asked me what was happening to her. I had no answer. She looked at me as if she couldn't believe there was none. "Am I dying?" she asked. I could only sit there. I couldn't tell her. She was perspiring. Her thin, stringy hair was stuck to her forehead. Her eyes were frightened, near tears.

I couldn't stand it when she cried. It tore my heart out every time she and Dad would fight, and she'd start crying. She didn't do it very often. Kept it bottled up. And it was usually over money. She'd want to buy us something, maybe new Easter clothes. He'd say we didn't have any money. She'd threaten to order it anyway. He'd say he would take her credit cards away. She'd come running into the family room, crying and blowing her nose with the Kleenex she always kept handy in the waistband of her pedal pushers. She'd say she was only doing it for us kids. We were too young to know what was going on, so Dad was always the bad guy. He'd come into the dining room and our hard stares would chase him away.

As I sat there, she began to cry. I couldn't handle it. I started to leave. She touched my arm. She never did that.

"It's for the best, you know."

"No, you'll get better," I said. "It'll be okay."

"No, it won't. You don't understand. You have your friends. Your job. A wife. Your whole life. I don't have anything."

"You've got Dad. The cats." It sounded pretty empty.

"But I don't have you kids. When your brother finally moved out, that was it. You were all gone. Do you know how lonely that was?"

"But we were always around. We came to visit. We had Christmas and Easter."

"But you weren't here for me every day anymore. I couldn't take care of you. Couldn't watch out for you. That's what I lived for, you know. Now it's gone and I'm alone. I just don't want to live anymore."

"Come on, Mom. You can't just give up. You've got reasons to live. I know you do." It was weak, but it was the best I could offer.

"You just don't know how lonely it can be. You've always been independent, a loner. You can handle it. I can't. And I don't want to anymore."

There was nothing more I could say. And then she died. Just closed her eyes. And I left her, alone again.

I never had the dream again. But I would see her alone. Passed out, alone. Waking up, alone. Inside herself, alone. I couldn't understand it. *She had a full life*, I thought. Or convinced myself. There were always people around, even after she'd pissed them off. They loved her and cared deeply about her. Yet she was completely alone. And she died that way.

I guess it's really a lonely world. Someone once said you can die from loneliness as surely as you can die from heart disease. I remember a writer commenting that it was not possible for two people to truly know each other. No matter how close the husband and wife, the father and son, the lover and beloved, we are all locked inside ourselves, which says something horrible about our lack of knowledge, about our hopeless and terrible, and sadly permanent loneliness. And something about the loneliness of the individual trying to find meaning in their isolation.

I guess when all us kids moved away, she just gave up. She had no reason to live anymore. The coroner's report listed heart failure. But my mom really died from the absoluteness of loneliness.

The Giants went on to lose in the ninth. And I lost it in the bar bathroom.

Image by Filipp Efanov. © 123RF.com.

"Broken Wing"

It was a leaden summer's day, threatening rain. The thunderheads pressed down on my shoulders.

The parents were gone. But I wasn't alone.

She was the first to get a tattoo. A broken heart.

I changed into a red flannel robe to cover my nakedness and changed the music.

As we smoked dope, we listened to Buffalo Springfield's "The Hour of Not Quite Rain."

As we made love, we listened to John Mayall's "Broken Wing."

She was my first lover. I was hers. We were both rank amateurs.

When she left, it was okay. I wanted to be alone.

We would see each other off-and-on over the years. We would come together to make love because we knew the other was just fine with that. No strings, no expectations. Just easy and comfortable.

When so many of us left town, she stayed behind. We'd see each other during school breaks.

I was living out of town when it ended.

As she shot herself up with heroin, she listened to Neil Young's "The Needle and the Damage Done."

Her baby girl lay nearby. She went into the bedroom closet and blew her brains out with a shotgun. A good friend we all went to high school with, then a policeman, found her. Unrecognizable except for her driver's license. And the broken heart.

I remember it all today as vividly as yesterday as I listen to Buffalo Springfield's "Sad Memory."

"Happy Trails"

The analog marquee fronting the Holiday Inn reads: "WILD WEST FILM FESTIVAL."

Inside, the hotel lobby and meeting rooms are filled with memorabilia, autograph tables, arts and crafts, souvenirs, food, and celebrities. The white hats, black hats, redskins, damsels-in-distress, and second bananas of countless Hollywood "oaters." All recognizable through the gray and wrinkles.

Roy Rogers shakes hands. He wears his trademark white, cowboy hat. Fringed and sequined cowboy shirt. Red, white, and blue eagle cowboy boots. The All-American Hero. With that easy smile. He flashed it and all the world was safe. Even from a Russian A-bomb.

I'm the next in line. I step up to face Roy.

"Got all your movies on video," I say.

"Well, buckaroo, my accountant appreciates that," Roy replies.

"You were my baby-sitter for a lot of Saturday mornings."

"Looks like we did a good job."

"Could sleep nights because you and Gene and Hopalong were watching out for me. Never prayed to God. Prayed to you."

"God shoots straighter."

"Wanted my father to be you."

"If wishes were horses, then beggars would ride."

"What kind of a man shows you how to pee on a fire, but never lets you win? Anything."

"Pard, a cowboy who tells the truth always has one foot in the stirrup."

"You raised a large family. Adopted lots of kids. They all turned out. What's the secret?"

Rory, my girlfriend, appears at the end of the table.

"A good woman," Roy says, noticing Rory.

"Old man blew that one out of the gate," I say.

"A sense of humor."

"Lost that when we were born."

"And patience. Lots and lots of patience."

"Strike three. Drove my brother off. Then me."

"A boy's struggle with his father makes him a man," Roy points out.

"That makes me Superman."

"What's your name, son?"

"Kevin."

Roy signs an 8X10 glossy of him and Trigger and Bullet.

"You want his approval?"

"Yes."

"Make him a grandfather. I wager he'll surprise you."

Roy gives me the photograph.

"Mind if I get a picture?" I ask.

Roy stands. I come around the table.   Rory snaps the camera.

"You are your father," Roy says.

"Know that."

I shake Roy's hand.

"Potty break. Good thing I don't ride anymore. My bladder's in worse shape than old Nellybelle."

Roy touches the brim of his hat and leaves.

I look at the signed photograph. The dedication reads: "To Kevin – A father is just a man, not a hero. Cut him some slack. Happy Trails, Roy Rogers."

"Spring Training"

In March 1962, our little black-and-white television continued to beam in world events. I followed the Giants in the newspaper and got back into my school and home routines. A young folk singer named Bob Dylan released his first album on Columbia Records, simply calling it, *Bob Dylan*. The first Kmart store opened in Garden City, Michigan. Wilt Chamberlain of pro basketball's Philadelphia Warriors scored one hundred points against the New York Knicks. The citizens of St. Louis voted to build a new baseball stadium for the Cardinals. U.S. military advisors began training South Vietnamese helicopter pilots. Because the Jack Tar Harrison Hotel had a "no black policy," the Philadelphia Phillies moved to Rocky Point Motel, twenty miles outside Clearwater, Florida, for Spring Training. In the 24th NCAA Men's Basketball Championship, Cincinnati beat Ohio State 71-59. Boxer Benny Paret died from injuries suffered during his bout with Emile Griffith at Madison Square Garden. Jack Paar hosted his last *The Tonight Show* on NBC. And Cesar Chavez founded the United Farm Workers Union.

It was a very long winter. Wet, cold, and foggy. I couldn't wait for spring. And baseball. Finally, the first Spring Training games rolled around. I stepped out the backyard gate and into Pike Park. I wrapped my fingers around the brand-new Rawlings baseball and held it up to the misty sun. I was filled with wishful thinking.

In 1962, the Yankees moved their Grapefruit League facilities from St. Petersburg's Al Lang Field to Ft. Lauderdale Stadium in Ft. Lauderdale, Florida. Their new stadium cost $600,000. It could seat

8,000 and even had air-conditioning, which nobody had back then. By moving to the east coast of Florida, the Yankees were closer to four other teams, which they could now play without having to travel so far. The Baltimore Orioles were in Miami, the Los Angeles Dodgers were in Vero Beach, the Washington Senators were in Pompano Beach, and the Kansas City Athletics were in West Palm Beach. The first workout for Yankee pitchers and catchers was February 19. The first full-squad workout was February 28. The first game was March 10 against the Baltimore Orioles.

The Giants also had a spanking new facility. It was located in the middle of nowhere, outside a place called Casa Grande in Arizona. Owner Horace Stoneham had built a $2 million resort designed to be a self-contained complex. It had its own airstrip, eighteen-hole championship golf course, pool, and multi-field complex with an adjoining ballpark that could seat 3,000. Stoneham built the facility to be used as a training complex in February and March, and a luxury resort hotel the rest of the year. The Giants opened 1962 in Tucson against the Cleveland Indians.

As the old saying goes, "hope springs eternal." And it did. Every March.

"Doctors' Daughters"

The rectangle of blue reflected the noonday sun.

The sweat dripped off my nose. I put the book down, walked to the edge of the pool, and dove in. I surfaced and smelled summer, colored with satisfaction.

I finally had my own pool. The pool I had always envied, had always drooled over as I stared through the sliding glass doors of my better-off-than-me friends' houses, face pressed against the glass. The kind of pool reserved for doctors' daughters.

I grew up with several girls who were the daughters of local doctors. They were all cute and smart. All braces, pink lipstick, ponytails. And unavailable. To someone like me. I was the oldest of five, the son of a phone company lifer and a homemaker. The girls all had nice houses and beautiful pools. In the college neighborhood. On streets with names like Princeton and Yale.

Now I lived on Wellesley.

I never got the doctor's daughter, but I got her daddy's pool.

Photograph by Vanston Shaw.

"The Mud Bowl"

In Memoriam: Kevin Clark, George Rogers, Don de Camp, and Brad Bassi.

They were old enough to know better. These over-60 victims of fate. But that didn't stop them. From playing a game in the rain. Like they had each year for the past 50 years.

It started on a Thanksgiving morning at Roosevelt and Pike Park. Then moved to Thousand Oaks, now Kewin. A group of Baby Boomers gathered to play "The Mud Bowl." It was a morning of glory in a rushing stream of unremarkable days. Adolescence run wild in lives of quiet desperation. And a way to avoid putting away those young boy ways. For just one day. It started out as a game. Then it became an excuse. For these "boys of autumn" to never grow up.

They'd been told for years by their parents, wives, girlfriends, and sibs to act their age. But did they listen? No way. They just drank more, smoked more, swore more, played harder, and did more stupid things. What would you expect from a bunch of guys with nicknames like Dancing Bear, Whitey, Putz, Goat, Bo're, Fast Johnny, Pancho, Hands, T Honey, and Pig?

In the beginning, it was about coming home from college during Thanksgiving break to catch up. They picked sides. Argued over rules. Played some touch that quickly turned into tackle. No plays. Everyone just went long. Then stayed up all night, after eating way too much turkey, to drink, play a little poker, and razz one another about how it was going with grades, girls, and life.

Then, it was about introducing wives and significant others and sharing pictures of new children, homes, cars, and jobs. They divided teams into "Class of '66" versus "The Other Guys." And canonized the gathering with T-shirts, a banquet the night before, a memorable (or was it memorial?) highlight video, trophies, and team photos. Real plays were sketched out on note cards. Tackle turned into flag football, so nobody got hurt. Although a few did. Teeth, ankles, knees. And the local TV stations came out because it was better than covering soup kitchens. Then bird, cocktails, and cards. The same old routines and sarcastic digs as the years piled on.

And now, it's about memories. They make catch-up phone calls and send emails from homes scattered across the West. Look at the photos and watch the videos alone and together. Remember those who are gone. And recall what each of them had done and not done and still hoped to do. A little less turkey, a lot less alcohol, and no poker.

They have passed the torch – AKA the "Cheap Shot Chicken" – to the next generation. And the generation after that. To carry on.

As long as there are two players still standing, there will always be a game.

The Mud Bowl was, and always will be, about old friends. And like Thanksgiving, it's about family and tradition. And boys playing a game in the mud.

To see the greatest hits of The Mud Bowl through the years, go to www.youtube.com/playlist?list=PL1DC1D27DE02B3FAD.

All the Mud Bowl buddies
Gather 'round tonight
Yesterday's alive and kicking
One more year
So we talk about some old times
And drink ourselves some beers
Still crazy after all these years
Still crazy after all these years

"Birth Order"

Dedicated to my sibs.

Kevin visits his father in the hospital. Tim Senior drowses. He looks thin and very tired. Kevin straightens up his father's room. It wakes his father.

"How you doing, Daddy-O?"

"Not bad."

"Joan holding up?"

"She's a tough old bird."

"Like you," Kevin says. "I'll check in with her later."

"I'd like that. She sort of gets lost in the shuffle."

"We need to watch that."

Kevin sits beside his father. He adjusts the plastic ID band on his Father's wrist. He lays his forearm next to his Father's forearm. He compares their palms, fingers, hands, arms, and skin. Cut from the same cloth.

"She's a good person, Kevin. She's been great for me. I just wish you kids would acknowledge that once-in-a-while."

"We can do that."

Kevin notices some needlepoint on the table beside the bed.

"You been working on that?" Kevin indicates the needlepoint.

"Not really. Not enough energy."

"Who's it for?"

"A Christmas present."

Tim closes his eyes a moment, gathering his strength. Kevin picks up the needlepoint and unrolls it. A photograph has been silk-screened onto the fabric. Pinned to the corner of the fabric is the original photograph he's working from. It's an old photo of the Woodworth family. Everyone is in it, including Kevin's mother and Sally, his estranged half-sister. Kevin catches his breath.

"That was the day after our little trip to the foothills," Tim says. Kevin nods.

There is a deeply sad look in his father's eyes. Tim closes his eyes again. Kevin takes his father's hand. His father opens his tired eyes and fights falling asleep.

"Has Grampa Otto been by?"

Tim shakes his head.

"Does he know?"

Tim shakes his head again.

"Think it's time I go see him."

A look of mild panic flashes through Tim's eyes. He grabs Kevin's hand.

Just then, two nurses enter.

"We need to run a few tests. Routine," the head nurse says.

"Was just leaving."

"We won't be long."

Kevin extricates his hand from his father's and pats his hand. Tim's eyes close. Kevin leaves his father lying alone, surrounded by equipment and strangers.

At a local coffee house, Kevin and Gary sip coffee.

"We're so much alike," Kevin says. "I knew exactly how he was feeling. It was almost as if I were looking out his eyes. He was scared. God, he looked so alone."

"We come in alone, we live alone, we go out alone," Gary replies.

"When he went to sleep, he was sure he was going to come out on the other side."

"He will."

"Shouldn't have left. Should have stayed. As usual, I did what worked for me."

"There's nothing you could do."

"I could be there for him. Like he's been there for me my entire life."

"But you were there. And he knows it."

"Should be worried about him, but I'm not. Just going on about my business. Doing stuff."

"Easy, Trigger, easy."

"Was thinking as I stood there, he's the last link to our immediate history. Mom's already gone. If he dies, he'll take our collective memory with him. He's the only one who remembers what's happened in our lives. Every little event. After he's gone, if I want to know about anything that's ever happened, especially when we were kids, there won't be anyone to ask. All those stories. He knows all the memories by heart. When he's gone, it's all gone. And we'll be left to reconstruct them as best we can."

In the ICU, Kevin, his brothers and sisters, stand in a half-circle around their father's bed. Kevin looks from face to face. He suddenly realizes they're standing in birth order. Oldest to youngest. Except for Sally, the eldest half-sister.

Funny, he thinks to himself. *We always stand in this order when we stand together.*

Kevin flashes on a photograph of the family taken during some long-forgotten Valentine's Day. Mother and Father stand in front of their children. And the children stand in birth order, facing their parents, each holding a hand-made paper valentine.

"Round and Round"

Round and round and round we spin,
To weave a wall to hem us in.
It won't be long.
It won't be long.
– Neil Young, "Round and Round"

Sex, Drugs, and Rock 'N Roll. Rock 'N Roll we got. Sex we were starting to get. Drugs we didn't

have a clue. We were the virgins, the newbies, the rookies. My best friend and me. He was cautious. I was

curious. We both had a very strong sense of self-preservation. And fear.

We went to Berkeley to change that. To score some mescaline from a high school classmate who'd

chosen Cal over JC. We listened to Neil Young's solo album which had just come out. He sang "The

Loner" as our connection explained the ins and outs.

How slow and slow and slow it goes,
To mend the tear that always shows.
It won't be long.
It won't be long.

Back home in the Valley, we went to our friend Chuck's house. That is, his

parent's house. He'd been in the Navy. He'd gotten out on a mental. He knew more than

we did. But he'd been damaged along the way. He hadn't had sufficient fear.

Captain Trips and the pros dropped by. The gang of addicts in training. The ones with no fear. To show us the dos and don'ts.

We locked ourselves in, closed the shades, and took off on a magic carpet ride. Joyriding to the edge; drag-racing to the cliff.

Lying on my back in the backyard, the edges of the trees spun like pinwheels on fire. Starry, starry night.

Inside the house, I popped Buffalo Springfield's "Greatest Hits" into the 8-track. The metallic blue guitar of "On the Way Home" punched holes in the walls.

It's a fine line between here and there, this side and the other. A very fine line.

How the hours will bend
through the time that you spend
till you turn to your eyes,
And you see your best friend
looking over the end
and you turn to see why,
And he looks in your eyes and he cries.

The next day, my brother came by with his girlfriend. He wanted the Buffalo Springfield 8-track I'd promised him and forgotten about. I slipped it through a slight crack in the front door, wondering why he was there so damned early. The sun, burning directly overhead, scorched my dark-adjusted eyes.

My friend went home. He couldn't face his family. He came back. He freaked out.

Captain Trips and the pros were called back to talk him down. They did. Eventually.

We never looked at things the same again.

Round and round and round we spin,
To weave a wall to hem us in,
It won't be long.
It won't be long.
– Neil Young, "Round and Round"

"Time Machine"

Dedicated to Douglas Spaulding.

Close your eyes and rock back on your shoe heels,
Let's thread time on a human spinning wheel;
Through veils of blue turning a weathered loom,
Weaving away cobwebs that come too soon
To cover our eyes and hide our wide smiles
With fears and pain and comfortable lies.
Following feelings your folks left behind,
Visions captured in Dandelion Wine;
Stand until you can hear the shifting dust,
Then start the wall clock before it can rust.
Careful what you do, careful what you say
Old and tired and hasn't moved all day.

> Time is all and nothing,
> for it lives in the mind of man;
> A time machine is nothing
> more than the memories of an old man.

Children are welcome, the old ones don't know,
If they saw our very own time machine,
They would smile and their cold logic would show;
All that their forsaken dark eyes can see
Of the far-traveling game we've now found,
Are the rocking gray eyes of the Colonel,

The oldest old man in tiny Green Town.
But for the child with dreams his daily wine
And innocent wonder his daily bread,
The Colonel can take you far back in time
With new stories of the never-be-dead,
Unraveling inside his graying head.

We will travel here, there and back again;
From a Boston Theater 1910
To hunting brown bison with Pawnee Bill
Far beyond the sacred Dakota Hills
And a rumbling coal black funeral train
Making its last lonely run full of pain.
To a war with neither colors nor sides
And scars that are impossible to hide.
If the old man closes his tired eyes
He's only recharging his batteries
Indian vision is what he will share
It is fooling time for those who would dare
Who really needs a Happiness Machine
When you can ride the one true Time Machine

      Time is all and nothing,
              for it lives in the mind of man;
     A time machine is nothing
               more than the memories of an old man.

The man with the scythe and the hourglass
Is out to shatter the mirror of dreams;
But we must stop the shifting sands of time
With miracles visible but not seen.
Cinnamon dusts and fine wine airs are weaved
Like spider webs traces around your eyes;
Pure happiness awaits if you believe
That long hot summers will always survive.
You can come on board any time at all.
But when you return to the arms of time
Remember journeys are easy for you
But lonely for the kind man left behind.

      Time is all and nothing,
              for it lives in the mind of man;

A time machine is nothing
    more than the memories of an old man.

As we left the extended care home and walked to the car, I asked my nephew if he'd ever done any time-traveling. He was young enough to want to but getting old enough to realize the difference between fact and science fiction. He replied with a hesitant, questioning "no." Well, you just did, I replied to a face of confusion. Your great-grandfather sitting in that rocking chair. When he tells you stories of his life, talks of things he once knew, he's transporting you into the past. The light was beginning to flicker behind my nephew's eyes. I know he's taken you to the Civil War, marching by his father's side at the Battle of Bull Run. I even think you rode in the back of a Conestoga wagon, sleeping next to him and the rest of the family, as they crossed the plains to California. Fighting Indians, watching people die from smallpox and animals from lack of water and food. You worked the gold mines of Sonora. You saw Three-Fingered Jack and Joaquin Murrieta as your great-grandmother served them lunch in her café. She remembered them as generous, kind men. Robin Hoods of the Sierra, not the murderous thieves as painted by Wells Fargo. You rode with Black Jack Pershing in Mexico and again in World War I. You survived the Great Depression and three more wars. World War II, Korea, and the Vietnam Conflict. You see, you are a time traveler, like Orwell predicted. Like Michael J. Fox. Except your time machine isn't a modified DeLorean or a Rube Goldberg contraption. Yours is made of flesh and blood. It has eyes and a voice. Most of all, it has a memory. He's passing it on to you, so you can pass it on to your children. That's how storytelling began and how it will continue.

Continuity and tradition and generations. Just different words for friends and family. It's an important part of our lives. To be able to look into the eyes of a great-grandmother or gaze at the fading photo of a great-grandfather and see yourself is to realize the thread that connects us all. It's sons of fathers who are brothers and friends, who once were grandsons and will someday be grandfathers. It's seeing a nephew or your best friend's son brought home from the hospital then suddenly finding him playing third base for your softball team. It's watching the son of a drug-overdosed drummer playing drums with his dad's old band at a record label's forty-year anniversary celebration jam session. To avoid it, deny it, to run and hide from it is to reject who you are, what you are, where you came from. To turn your back on it is to cut yourself loose from your moorings, your stabilizers. It'll make you crazy. And it'll make you alone and lonely.

"Hard Candy"

It's not even Halloween and my sister is listening to Bing sing "White Christmas." Her trees and lights will be up soon. And I won't be far behind. Our family loves Christmas. Always has. Thanks largely to our mother, who took refuge in Christmas. She truly believed:

Oh, why can't every day be like Christmas
Why can't that feeling go on endlessly
For if every day could be just like Christmas
What a wonderful world this would be
– Elvis Presley, "If Every Day Was Like Christmas"

She loved giving presents, even though we couldn't afford them. My dad would battle the debt she ran up at Christmas for the rest of the year. But it made her happy and that made him happy.

Every year, she would buy ribbon candy, solid hard candy, and chewy candy filled with fruit, even though she was overweight and diabetic. Hell, it was Christmas. She could lose weight after New Year's.

Then the sadness would blanket her. And she'd start drinking. The holidays are hard enough without your mother being drunk most of the time.

They say drinking and driving don't mix. They can certainly say the same about the holidays. You should never drink and reminisce.

My most vivid memories of her at Christmas are the initial euphoria of the spirit of Christmas, then the distilled spirits, then the abuse, then the fears, then the spirits of Christmases past, then her passed out in her chair or puking in the middle of the night.

A lot of people numb the holidays with alcohol. It's tough when it happens to anyone. But it's really bad if it's a woman, especially your mother.

I don't miss the hard candy.

"Devil Dog"

It got to the point where we didn't see it anymore. I guess that's the way it is with tattoos.

My father's arms and my arms were pretty much the same. I especially realize that now as I get older and I'm closer in age to his when I was growing up. As I gaze at his left arm lying flat against the card table, suiting his pinochle cards, I recall sitting on his lap and staring at the bulldog with the spiked collar and the furled banner that read: "United States Marine Corps." It took some serious prodding, or a little alcohol, to get him to tell stories about the war in the Pacific. He didn't like talking about it. He went in at 17-and-a-half and came out much older. His father accepted his high school diploma while he was in a foxhole in Saipan.

"This is my rifle, this is my gun," he would repeat the chant he learned in basic training to distinguish between the two. "This is for shooting, this is for fun." He chuckled as he recalled his fellow recruits forced to walk through camp holding their penis when they forgot the difference between the two. He didn't smile as much when he would talk about going out on patrol with those in his squad who wanted to do a little souveniring. My dad was a natural leader and was quickly called upon to lead others. He frowned when he told us about one of his men puking his guts out when the bloated corpse of a Japanese soldier, who had been burned alive by a flamethrower, cracked open and oozed yellow goo, as the peach-fuzzed grunt tried to remove the dead man's samurai sword.

My father was a member of the greatest generation. Young men who were called upon to do things that were often less than great. The tattoo was cool, but not what it represented. He wasn't always proud of what he had done. And he was reminded of it every day as he stared at the fading ink of the Devil Dog.

Image by Brot Mandel. © 123RF.com.

"Dylan"

You like potato and I like potahto,
You like tomato and I like tomahto
Potato, potahto, Tomato, tomahto,
Let's call the whole thing off
– George and Ira Gershwin, "Let's Call the Whole Thing Off"

Boys and girls together. Hormones erupting. We had gathered in the living room of Cathy's house to listen to the Womenfolk, a trio of high school classmates who wanted to be folksingers. Janis was the ringleader, the passionate one. Julia was the one I was passionate about. Sherry was there for the harmony. The Wild Men, another trio of guy classmates and friends, were there to listen and wait their turn.

We talked about Friday's football game against Downey, the obligatory post-game gathering at Hob Nob Pizza, and the float our two "Y" groups were collaborating on for homecoming. I eyed Julia as they sang. She smiled a sweet, crooked smile. I could still smell her perfume on my sweater. The song ended. We applauded.

"That was 'Blowin' in the Wind,'" Janis said. "By Bob Dylan." She pronounced it like Matt Dillon.

"No, it's Dylan," I corrected, pronouncing it like *Dialin' for Dollars* and pointing at his name on the album cover. I was always a bit of a contrarian. It was fun. Sort of like punching the girl you liked when you were in kindergarten. Flirtatious taps.

"It's Dylan," Janis countered, getting frustrated. "Like the poet Dylan Thomas."

"Better buy an amp," I said. "The times they are a-changin.'"

"Man, those folkies were pissed off," said Alan, the front Wild Man. "Newport never sounded so radical."

"It sounded cool," Warren added, the tallest and oldest of the Wild Men. "'Like a Rolling Stone' all shot up with electric guitars and drums. Truly awesome."

"He sold out," Janis said. "That's why those people were so upset."

"They don't like change, I guess," said sweet, sweet Julia.

Dylan had altered the course of music. Yet again. He shocked the 1965 Newport Folk Festival by plugging in with Al Kooper and Michael Bloomfield and the music scene would never be the same. The Folkies were about to enter Sunburst Stratland. And they weren't happy about it.

Dylan truly was our troubadour. Our canary in the coal mine. He spoke the Truth, with a capital "T." I was not that big a fan. I was into old time rock 'n roll, like the Everly Brothers. And the new stuff by the Killer Bs – the Beach Boys, the Beatles, the Byrds, and Buffalo Springfield. I hated Dylan's voice, but his lyrics were pure poetry. They inspired me. They inspired the nation. They inspired the world. They inspired a generation to sing, to write, to act, to get involved. We did. And we changed some things. Some.

I listen to *Highway 61 Revisited* and am still blown away. I watch the movie *I'm Not There* and realize he was, and is, a true Force of Destiny. I attend a concert at the Stockton Arena where he plays some of his old stuff wrapped in a new package. It still works. He can still bring it. And it's great to see all those old Folkies come out of the Woodstock to worship their God.

I pop "Just Like Tom Thumb's Blues" into the CD player and I see all those fresh-faced kids standing around the piano in the Spanish-style home on Magnolia Avenue on a fall Saturday in Modesto circa 1965. They were thinking about music. I wasn't. They were in love with the music. I was in love with Julia.

Janis never felt the same about Dylan or me again.

You say yes, I say no
You say stop and I say go, go, go
Oh, no
You say goodbye and I say hello
Hello, hello
– Lennon and McCartney, "Hello Goodbye"

"Christmas Star"

They sat on the curb across the street like three jaybirds with the thick tule fog swirling around them. Not talking, not pointing, just staring. Transfixed by my Christmas tree, all lit up in the living room window, with the bright star on top.

They were homeless. They had nowhere to go. But, for a moment, the tree took them back to a time and place when they were somebody else. When Christmas was a celebration, not a day on the calendar for the shelter to serve turkey with all the trimmings.

I felt sorry for them and realized how lucky I was. To have had a wonderful childhood, a caring family, a loving wife, great friends, and a supportive community so that Christmas truly was the most wonderful time of the year.

I thought about offering them something – food, drink, a gift, but I realized that might embarrass or offend them. Instead, I opened the curtains wider.

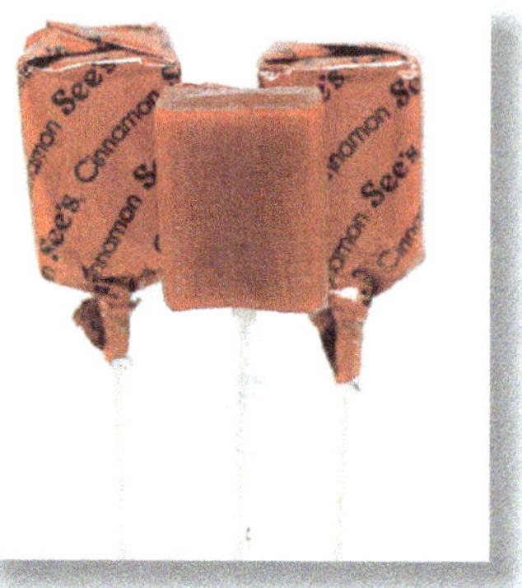

"Cinnamon Sucker"

I can never smell cinnamon without conjuring the little corner store next door to my buddy John Hart's house. He's the guy who pushed me down and chipped my front tooth.

The store was on the way to and from Garrison Elementary School, where we both attended third grade. Those kids, whose parents gave them money for treats, always stopped on their way home to buy something sweet. It might have been Bazooka bubble gum, plastic lips filled with sweet sugar water, Three Musketeers, Paydays, and cinnamon suckers.

The sucker was a square block of dark, reddish-brown sugar on a white cardboard stick. I think it was made by See's. You slid it into your mouth, rolled it off to one side, and sucked on it until it was glued to the inside of your cheek.

For me, it was a luxury. My parents couldn't afford to give us any extra money. The only way I could ever taste that sucker was if a friend bought me one, or a buddy let me have a lick, or finish it off when they were tired of it. We didn't think too much about swapping slobbers back then, especially when it was something so good.

The only other time I had my own cinnamon sucker was when I slipped one into my jeans pocket while I was hanging out at the little neighborhood store near the railroad tracks by Roosevelt Junior High. My father caught me when he noticed the white stick protruding from my lips. He marched me back to the store, gave me the money to pay for the sucker, and made me apologize. I was mortified, but I never did it again. Lesson learned.

The other day, I saw those very same suckers in a mom-and-pop convenience/liquor/gas station run by Indian or Pakistani immigrants. I bought two. One for me and one for the little street urchin wandering the aisles looking for his mother.

Iron Roses by Susan Church.

"Generations"

Corinne gave the only thing she had to give. Herself. She had a baby girl. She wasn't married. She never saw the father again. She gave the baby up for adoption. She found a man who loved her. They had five children, three boys and two girls. She tried to teach her children, especially the girls, to be their own person. But she didn't lead very well by her own example.

Her oldest daughter had trouble with men. She talked one out of raping her. She ran away to Los Angeles with another. She took another to court for abuse and lost. Like mother, like daughter. She found a man who loved her. They had two children, two girls. She named the oldest Corinne. She tried to teach her girls to respect themselves. But she didn't lead very well by her own admission.

Her oldest daughter had trouble with men. She followed one to Los Angeles. She gave the one true thing she had to give. Herself. Like grandmother, like mother, like daughter. Now, she's pregnant.

It's a girl.

"White Christmas"

In the movie, *The Bishop's Wife*, there is a scene between the Professor and Julia inside Maggenti's flower shop. After haggling with Maggenti over the price per branch of a Christmas tree, the Professor becomes wistful and says, "I like to have a Christmas tree because it reminds me of my childhood. I find, for some good reason, that this is a good time of year for looking backward. Can you imagine me ever having been a child?"

My mother was so much the child at Christmas that she had two trees. A living green tree in the family room and an artificial, 1960s silver Alcoa in the living room. Each year, when Christmas was over, she would ask my dad to plant the green tree outside the family room window so she could continue to enjoy it until it turned dead brown.

Like most families, our Christmases were a collection of rituals. It always began with stringing the large, multi-colored bulbs around the house exterior. It wasn't engineer precise, but it was festive. And staking out a flat plastic Santa in his sleigh and eight tiny reindeer on the front lawn. Then the Alcoa landed, and the green tree was purchased and installed and covered with old and new ornaments, one of which featured the smiling face of country singer Slim Whitman. But that's another story. These ceremonies would be followed by the baking of peanut butter, chocolate chip cookies and the making of my dad's classic fudge. Mom would purchase her favorite fruit-filled and ribboned hard candy that always ravaged someone's tooth. We'd write our letters to Santa, mark the gifts we wanted in the Sears and Penny's catalogues, and visit the basement of the downtown Sears store, which was transformed each year into Santa's Toyland. My youngest little sister, Cindy – AKA Sammy – remembered that the Sears & Roebuck "Wish Book" always arrived in brown paper. She would use a Bic pen to circle and circle the things she wanted until the circle was imprinted on the pages below. It really didn't matter how many times she circled her wishes because Mom bought us pretty much everything we asked for. Her childhood Christmases had been pretty bleak, so she wanted to make sure ours weren't.

And then the Santa games would begin. As the oldest, I became the first non-believer. My next oldest brother, Tommy, and I would start looking for the gifts our parents had squirreled away. In closets, in drawers, under beds, in the garage. And we'd try not to leak the deflating truth to our younger sibs. They religiously continued to put out milk and cookies for Santa and Santa always ate and drank whatever we left him. On Christmas morning, for some strange reason, Dad just couldn't eat another cookie. Sammy remembers Mike Cannizzaro, Tommy's father-in-law, playing pinochle on Christmas Eve with our folks and threatening to start a fire. Sammy was on the verge of realizing that Santa was a myth, but she still made sure there was no fire that night before she went to bed to dream of sugar plums.

Inevitably, my father would have to assemble something each year. The directions were horrible, usually written by someone in Taiwan, Hong Kong, or the Philippines, and the "toddy for the body" didn't help. From bicycles to cardboard kitchens, he put them all together on countless Christmas Eves. As I got older, I helped. And I passed the responsibility down to Tommy and then to my next youngest brother, Wendy.

One Christmas, I remember rousting Tommy, who was 15 months younger than me, out of bed, scurrying down the hallway, and peeking through the hallway door into the kitchen where my dad was busy wrapping gifts on the gray Formica table. I recall with a smile the year he tried to wrap our football helmets. My oldest little sister, Debbie, still remembers the breathless anticipation we all experienced when Mom made us wait in our rooms, so the parents could get their coffee, pry their eyes open, have a cigarette, and make sure everything was perfectly set up before we could burst into the wonderland of gifts. Only to be blinded by four, white-hot lights.

One holiday, my father had bought an 8-millimeter camera with a light bar to capture the festivities. The lights were so bright, every movie featured people squinting in pain, their hands thrown up to cover their faces. His footage was pretty much the same each year. Up the tree and down the tree. Then shots of presents piled under both trees. And close-ups of sleeping animals and dozing humans. One year, somehow, my father double-exposed the film. He must have forgotten that he had already recorded Christmas when he shot the family vacation to SeaWorld. When the film was developed, it featured dolphins and orcas dancing through the Alcoa.

For my family, Christmas was all about the music. It still is. I can never get enough of Bing singing "White Christmas," Brenda Lee's "Rockin' Around the Christmas Tree," or "Run Rudolph Run" by Keith Richards, or "Mary, Did You Know?" by Kenny Rogers. It was the quickest way to get into the spirit.

Plus, the movies. *Holiday Inn, White Christmas, The Bishop's Wife, A Christmas Carol*, and *It's a Wonderful Life*. And, over the years, like the music, more classics were added. *The Nutcracker*, twenty-four hours of *A Christmas Story*, a *Muppet Christmas Carol, National Lampoon's Christmas Vacation, thirtysomething Christmas, Scrooged, Love Actually*, and *The Family Stone*.

Then there were the gifts. The wonderful, every-kid-had-to-have-one presents, like the testosterone-fueled, hand-to-hand combat of the Rock 'Em Sock 'Em Robots; the eloquent, loquacious Chatty Cathy; or the very cool, just-like-the-movies 007 gadgets. There was athletic gear, like the full football uniforms we three boys got which, Wendy always reminded me, let Tommy and me whomp on him without getting into trouble. And my sisters' vanity sets, which were full-sized, hard plastic make-up tables with flip-up mirrors, little side drawers, and fake make-up. There were gifts that changed everything, like the year Wendy got his first guitar and amp. A Sears Silvertone. And who can ever forget the bright, shiny spokes of brand-new bikes flashing in the winter sun. Once all the presents were distributed, Sammy and Wendy would then stage their annual who-gets-to-open-the-last-present contest, with both tucking away at least one present to be "discovered" after everyone had opened their last gift.

And what would Christmas be without the food. Turkey stuffed with oyster dressing ground up in an old hand-cranked meat grinder. Dips that made our mouths water. Clam, onion, bacon. Crackers, chips, pretzels. A salt overdose. Eggnog, hot chocolate with marshmallows, Tom and Jerries. A sugar overload.

And the rest of the traditions. Mike Cannizzaro coming to the house dressed like Santa Claus and stealing presents from under our tree. Debbie making cowboy jackets and shirts for us older boys and my best friend, George, who had his own routine of making sugar-covered walnuts, which always seemed to have a shell or two left intact because he'd had a few too many Buds while making them. Singing Christmas Carols in our neighborhood and with our stepmom Jo's family after Mom passed away. Searching out creative stocking-stuffers for my wife Robin, my stepsons, and her family. Each year, we added more rituals. The *Nutcracker Suite* ballet at the San Francisco Opera House, *La Pastorela* at *El Teatro Campesino* in San Juan Bautista, Christmas in the Adobes in Monterey, the Modesto Symphony's Candlelight Concerts, the gift exchange at Tommy's house, cruising Christmas Tree Lane, decorating sugar cookies for Robin's cookie exchange, holiday open houses, and the Christmas parades in Twain Harte and Modesto.

They say Christmas is for kids. At this time of year, I often wish I were a kid again.

"Tyranny of the Downbeat"
Remembrances of Things Musical

It was twenty years ago today,
That Sergeant Pepper taught the band to play.
They been goin' in and out of style,
But they're guaranteed to raise a smile.
So let me introduce to you,
The band you've known for all these years,
– The Beatles, "Sergeant Pepper's Lonely Hearts Club Band"

There's a saying. Our mortality is measured by the celebrities we grow old with; that movies help mark out our lives. Do you remember who you were when you first saw *Casablanca*, *Citizen Kane*, or *2001*? It was true in the Forties and Fifties and perhaps it may still be today. For me, it wasn't the movies. It was the music. I remember exactly who I was and what I was doing by certain songs. And every time I hear one, I'm back to what I was then, at that moment. In the Sixties, music really did mark the time of our lives. All the events, all the experiences, all the memories from that time are linked forever to a mesmerizing melody or smashing power chord, a mobilizing lyric or communal chorus.

There's another saying. Everything is changeable. Only change is eternal. It is inevitable. It is persistent. As predictable as time. As tyrannical as the downbeat. The Sixties were a time for change and a time of change. And rock 'n roll provided our anthems.

Because I lived in the Central Valley, I wasn't always a part of what was happening in San Francisco – The City. So, I participated, vicariously, on my time machine – the radio.

It seems we always begin and end these travels with the same band. A group that kept that decade alive for thousands. The Grateful Dead started us down the golden road and a variation on a theme is still truckin' today.

But "The Herald" who signaled the real beginning of our trip was, appropriately enough, a music critic: Ralph J. Gleason, with a little back-up from Ben Fong-Torres and local disc jockeys. Some on AM, but most on the first underground, free-form, FM stations, like KMPX, then KSAN. It was "Big Daddy" Tom Donahue, or Creedence Clearwater Revival playing the long version of "Suzy Q" at a street dance. The official journal of the journey was not Gleason's *Chronicle*, but a "rock tabloid." A new publication that commented on the counterculture by writing about the music it made. *Rolling Stone*, a rag dedicated to printing "All the News That Fits."

Why fate chose The City as the location for this flowering of music and gathering of tribes will never be known. But it did. And it gave us an incredible amount of music and musicians. The Charlatans. Moby Grape. It's A Beautiful Day. The Beau Brummels. The Jefferson Airplane. The Steve Miller Band. Big Brother. The Youngbloods. I hear Quicksilver's "Pride of Man" and I think of Chet Helms and "The Family Dog."

The new children will live,
For the elders have died.
I wave good-bye to America,
And smile hello to the world.
– Tim Buckley, "Hello/Good-bye"

I remember the first "official" outdoor rock concert. "Magic Mountain" at Mt. Tamalpais in Marin. Tim Buckley backed by Carter C.C. Collins. I wondered if I should wear flowers in my thinning hair.

"Pushin' Too Hard." Sky Saxon and the Seeds. The first time I smoked dope. "The Loner." Neil

Young's first solo album and my first experience with psychedelics. We were all counter-culture cowboys, denim Indians like him. Fringed, buckskinned, and alone in our melancholy.

"Feel-Like-I'm-Fixin'-to-Die-Rag" will always be Vietnam and a long bus ride to Fresno for my induction physical. I was terminally healthy. Then, there was a longer trip to the Oakland Draft Resistance Center, knowing that if I didn't do something I was going to die. After all, when the numbers were called the night of the lottery, I was number twenty-four. Cannon fodder.

"Light My Fire." 1967. The Doors and Love in my hometown. They rocked the roller-skating rink. I was curious about the genesis of their name.

"Long Time Gone." 1969. CS&N rallying the crowd at the Polo Grounds in Golden Gate Park. They proved that music was the anthem of the marching, charging people. We walked out together, arm-in-arm.

There was a point when music and movies did come together. *Easy Rider* broke new ground in many ways. But I remember it especially as one of the first movies to really use rock 'n roll to help tell the story. "Born To Be Wild," "Ballad of Easy Rider," and "Don't Bogart that Joint." Reality at twenty-four frames per second.

Watching *Top Gun* again the other night, the latest rock 'n roll movie, I hear Tom Cruise say his mom's favorite song was Otis Redding's "Dock of the Bay." It's a little unsettling. We are now the parents we warned ourselves about. But it's really no surprise. It's predictable. Just like time. It's persistent. Just like change. And it's inevitable. Just like the downbeat.

Lately it occurs to me,
What a long, strange trip it's been.
– The Grateful Dead, "Truckin'"

"Palisades Park"

You'll never know how great a kiss can feel
When you stop at the top of a Ferris wheel
When I fell in love down at Palisades Park
– Freddy "Boom Boom" Cannon, "Palisades Park"

The best place to go on a date was the fair. Especially a first date. It didn't matter if it was the county fair or the state fair.

Hot summer nights, bright neon lights, hot dogs and corn dogs, games of chance and games of skill, rides that made you tingle and rides that made you vomit. The smells of the 4-H barns, the displays of handiwork and horticulture, and the carnies challenging your manhood. I always played the pinball machine horse-racing game. Each time you won, you got a different-sized horse. The ultimate prize was a horse clock. For her, I'd try to win a stuffed animal. I had a pretty decent arm, so I could knock over the leaded milk bottles and win a small, pink, furry creature of some sort.

It was all about possibilities. Infinite possibilities. What were the chances you would hold hands, get a kiss, decide to go steady, or get lucky? The names of the girls changed, but not the anticipation.

The fair was the one place you could go where her folks wouldn't freak. It was the one place where you could find a dark, secluded place like the Tunnel of Love and kiss her and touch her and smell her.

When I go to the fair today and walk those dusty, asphalt paths, eating a corn dog and drinking a beer, I can still feel how it felt to be stuck at the top of the Ferris wheel.

Photograph by James A. Ewing.

"Baseball and the Blues"

When Mr. Lowney was done giving us the lowdown on his baseball career, he turned to the blues.

He punctuated each pronouncement with a note or two on the harp. Happy and sad, upbeat and downbeat, fast and slow, cool and hot, and all the colors and flavors in between.

"There's nothing more American than baseball and the blues," he said. "Both were born on the backroads and in the backwaters and at the crossroads of the American continent. If you want to understand the heart and mind and soul of America, who we are as Americans, you need to know both." He gave a rapid-fire rundown of the long road they'd traveled together.

"Baseball and the blues were born to break your heart.

Baseball ain't nothin' but a good player tryin' not to be bad. The blues ain't nothin' but a good man feelin' bad.

Baseball opens in the spring when everything begins again. The blues have always been about new beginnings.

Baseball ends when the chill rains of fall come. The blues never end.

Baseball blossoms in the summer air and light. The blues are in full bloom just 'round midnight.

Baseball and the blues celebrate all the curves that life throws you.

We play baseball to lift our souls. We play the blues to bare our souls.

We play baseball to heal our hearts. We play the blues because our hearts have been hurt.

We play baseball to get home safe. We play the blues because we have no safe home to get to.

Baseball and the blues have a long memory.

In baseball and the blues, you fail more than you succeed. One for three gets you into the Hall of Fame.

In baseball, many are best remembered for their failures, not their successes. The blues celebrates that.

Baseball and the blues reflect our triumphs and defeats. When we're good, we're very good. When we're bad, there's nothing worse.

Baseball and the blues both make you suffer.

Baseball and the blues tell a lot of the same stories. About race, playing it straight and cheating, immigration, the tension between fathers and sons, acceptance, class warfare, alienation, labor and management, pop culture, myth, the individual and the crowd, and heroes.

In baseball and the blues, you can feel good and bad. Up and down. In and out. Fair and foul. Like a winner and a loser. Sometimes all at the same time.

We see our own daily lives reflected in the wins and losses, trials and tribulations of our baseball heroes. The blues sings songs about it.

Baseball and the blues are haunted by ghosts of who and what have gone before. Of past heroes and moments, of present successes, of future dreams.

Baseball and the blues are all about hope. Of a brighter day and a better tomorrow.

For baseball and the blues, practice sometimes makes perfect.

Baseball looks easy when it's done right. So does the blues.

They both fool us into thinking we've got it all figured out. Just before it all falls apart.

No one beats baseball or the blues for long.

In baseball and the blues, trouble happens.

And I love them both as dearly as the Valley loves the rain."

"Quality of Air"

There is always a fall day when you know summer is over. The tenor of the light, the timbre of the air. Everything looks and smells differently. Somehow thinner.

That means winter is just around the corner, panic attacks just around the bend.

I've never liked being cold and wet. And that's what the Valley in winter is all about. Bare trees and gray skies.

Although the end of summer means football, Halloween, Thanksgiving, Christmas, New Year's, and the Super Bowl, I'm never quite ready to see it go.

I've emptied the gun and booked my flight to Arizona. Leaving tomorrow.

"Wearin' o' the Green"

My mother never met a holiday she didn't like. Partly because each one was a day to celebrate. A day off from the day-to-day. Plus, they were all fun in their own way. One of her favorites was March 17th – St. Patrick's Day. It had nothing to do with being Irish because she was Bavarian German. Or drinking, although she enjoyed a cocktail or two. Or shamrocks, although she was terminally superstitious. Or leprechauns, though I think she believed they really existed and would have dearly loved to find the pot o' gold at the end of the rainbow. For *Madre*, it was all about the "wearin' o' the green."

If you didn't wear green on St. Patty's Day, she would pinch you. Not an easy pinch, but a turn-the-skin-red and leave-a-white-mark twister. She loved catching us kids without our green on. Because she always trapped us first thing in the morning, when we were still half-asleep, it was easy; easier than fooling us on April Fool's Day, but that's a different story. Of course, we'd be sure to add some green somewhere before we headed off to school, since every kid there had learned the same painful lesson at home, and each was eager to apply it to their classmates. When we finally donned the green, it was usually someplace invisible so we could trick our attackers, since turnabout was fair play if they were wrong. The pincher would thus become the pinchee.

I'm pretty sure Mom didn't know that the tradition originated with an Irish street ballad written in 1798. And that green, which was one of the colors of the Irish flag and the shamrock, represented the

Irish rebellion from the British Empire, whose national color was red, thanks to the Union Jack and their military uniforms. Because it became a sign of Irish patriotism, any Irishman caught wearing green was hanged on the spot by the Brits. I think if my mom had known the true history, she might have thought twice about threatening us with the dreaded pinch if we didn't wear the green. But, not likely. It tickled her too much.

As far as the pinching part of the tradition, that was purely an American invention, which reportedly started in the early 1700s. Those early colonials believed that wearing green made you invisible to leprechauns, who would pinch anyone they could see, which meant anyone not wearing green. Kind of a vicious circle. People began pinching those who didn't wear green as a reminder that the wee folk could see them, making them fair game, thus freeing the warner to sneak up and pinch the warnee before the little people did. It was silly, but fun.

Holiday superstitions and rituals. They dotted the calendar and filled our days, passed from generation to generation.

They continue, but they're not the same.

"The Acts of Love"

It's a young world
When you're in love, you're in a young world.
– "Young World," Written by Jerry Fuller, Performed by Ricky Nelson

First Love is confusing and exciting. Her name was Jill. We were classmates at Grace M. Davis High School. We spent most of the year together. Passing notes, decorating floats, eating lunch, going to games, hanging out at her house. We went to the Christmas formal. I remember smelling her perfume on my sweater during class. It made it hard to concentrate. All I wanted to do was be next to her. My priorities suddenly changed. Family and friends and Babe Ruth baseball faded away.

Young Love is gut-wrenching and heartburning. Her name was Kelly. We were undergrads at UC Davis. I met her in Paris while I was traveling, and she was a foreign exchange student. She was the younger sister of a high school buddy. We spent all my time in France together and carried on when we both returned to California. Going to movies, doing videos for a class project, riding bikes, studying, hanging out at her apartment. She was in love with someone else. All I wanted to do was hear her laugh. Priorities shifted. Family and friends and intramural softball were set aside.

Remember once before
Hearin' the old folks say
Love's an ageless old rhyme

But now a days you know
The sayin' depends so much on
The kind of woman that you find.
– "Kind Woman," Written by Richie Furay, Performed by Buffalo Springfield

Good Love Gone Bad is sad. Her name was Angela. We grew up blocks from each other. She was the younger sister of a girl I'd known since elementary school. We re-connected in college, courted, married, and moved to San Francisco then Honolulu. We spent a lifetime alone together. Dancing at clubs, working and acting out, chasing money, partying, hanging out at the beach. All I wanted to do was get away from her. Our priorities fell apart. Family and friends and city softball got lost in the shuffle.

Enduring Love is comforting and reassuring. Her name is Rory. We were both divorced and had returned home to Modesto. She was the younger sister of one of my best friends. I obviously have a thing about younger sisters. She had two sons. I had no children. We spent time together. Then we moved in together. Then we married. Travelling, raising her children, taking classes, volunteering, hanging out at home. All I wanted to do was be alone with her. Priorities transformed. Family and friends and senior softball were welcome again.

The many acts of love. It's a wonderful feeling. It's a confusing feeling. It's a hollow feeling. It's a contented feeling.

I hope I always feel that way.

At last
My love has come along
My lonely days are over
And life is like a song.
– "At Last," Written by Mark Gordon and Harry Warren, Performed by Etta James

"Opening Day"

Opening Day always meant the end of winter and the beginning of summer. (Although it really was spring.) The last of the season I hated and the first of the season I loved. Every true baseball fan couldn't wait for that special day. We'd all been marking off our calendars since the last pitch of last year's World Series. On Opening Day, we could live and breathe and hope again. On Opening Day, every team was in the race. Everyone was a contender.

As the first official franchise in Major League Baseball history, the Cincinnati Reds always got to be the first team to play on Opening Day. They held the "opening of the Openers." It was said that the citizens of the "Queen City" looked upon Opening Day as "one small notch below Christmas."

Since baseball was, after all, the national pastime, Opening Day always seemed to attract politicians anxious to show the American people they were one of them, had the right stuff, and could wing a fast ball up there with the best of them. President William Howard Taft, who was a big fan – in size and enthusiasm – was the first president to throw out the first pitch way back on April 14th, 1910. In 1950, Harry S. Truman, who happened to be ambidextrous, threw out balls both right-handed and left-handed. On April 9th, 1962, President John F. Kennedy continued the tradition by throwing out the first pitch at Washington's new District of Columbia Stadium. In more recent times, President George W. Bush threw out the first pitch for the Texas Rangers, a team he once owned.

Early Wynn, a Hall of Fame pitcher who played his entire career in the American League for the Senators, Indians, and White Sox, once said about Opening Day, "An opener is not like any other game. There's that little extra excitement, a faster beating of the heart. You have that anxiety to get off to a good start, for yourself and for the team. You know that when you win the first one, you can't lose 'em all." I liked his name and his optimism.

In 1962, Opening Day for the New York Yankees took place on April 10th against the Baltimore Orioles at Yankee Stadium. Mrs. Claire Ruth, The Babe's widow, threw out the first pitch. My team, the Giants, would be opening against the Milwaukee Braves at Candlestick Park on Candlestick Point in San Francisco later that day. The Yankees would almost be done by then. And I'd be listening to my heroes on my transistor radio tuned to KBEE 970-AM.

I had never attended any Opening Day games because it was too expensive, and my dad couldn't afford to take the day off. Plus, there were five of us kids, so he would have to decide who to take since he didn't have enough money to take us all. That was a "no-win" situation. But there were many other "Opening Days" that I did attend with my father. The Opening Day of each Little League and Babe Ruth season. And that's because my dad was my coach for just about all the teams I played for while attending elementary school, junior high, and high school.

To young boys, coaches were gods, mentors, teachers, and role models. If you were lucky, like me, that man was your father. In my experience, there were two kinds of coaches. Those who were quiet and led by example and those who yelled and tried to browbeat you into being better. I preferred the former, which was the kind of coach my dad was. I never responded to the coach who screamed red-faced at his players. I remember reading that Mickey Mantle hated Casey Stengel because the "Old Perfessor" was always riding him, which is what Mantle's father had done to him all his life. Mantle said they were never satisfied. That didn't stop him from trying to please them.

From our coaches, we learned about baseball, and we learned about life. We learned about preparation, attitude, and teamwork. We learned that talent is as much a result of practice and dedication as natural ability or instincts. We learned about being confident versus being cocky. About being gracious in victory, as well as defeat. About knowing before each play what you were going to do. And about backing up. The play and your teammates. We learned about taking something away from each win and loss, and then putting it all behind you. We also learned about mastering the mechanics of the game. About physical and mental conditioning. We learned about the history and tradition of the game. And about never giving up. On a game, on your teammate, on yourself.

In baseball and in life, I tried to please my dad, but not because he expected or demanded it. But because he won it. Quietly.

"On Opening Day, the world is all future. There is no past."
– *Lou Boudreau, American League Player and Manager*

"Artifacts"

My best friend's son and I played a round of golf last summer. It was the first time we had teed off since his father died. He inherited his father's clubs and golf bag. On the first tee, he unzipped one of the side pockets to put away his wallet. Inside was a water bottle and a half-full bag of sunflower seeds that hadn't been touched since the last time his father and I played.

When my mother-in-law died, we inherited a boom box her children had given her so she could listen to music without it becoming a bother. I put it on a shelf in the garage so I could play CDs and the Giants games while working in the yard. I decided to play some old Buffalo Springfield tunes. I opened the CD changer. It was filled with Christmas discs from the previous year. It was likely the last music she listened to.

That same Christmas, my wife and I had toured several homes as part of the "Holiday Open House" fund-raiser for Community Hospice. Each home offered refreshments. Some sold home-made gifts. Each house had its own unique collection of family memorabilia displayed on bookshelves, mantles, windowsills, pianos, and refrigerators. The refrigerators were especially interesting and revealing, with their collections of drawings, photos, report cards, coupons, lists, cartoons, reminders, and aspirations.

"Interesting, isn't it?" I said. "A room tells us so much about who we are."

"It is sweet," my wife added.

We moved past a dusty treadmill, and I said, "We display things that are important to us to prove we're more or less okay. That we make sense. That we have value. That we've been here."

"It is sad," she replied.

The clutter, all the things that are worn out, the things we meant to do, all reveal this brokenness in our lives. Photos, a few trophies, artwork, and some rare objects show our pride, our few shining moments.

"It's a little selfish," I said. "We collect all these things, but we're only borrowing them for a while. When we're gone, they go live with somebody else."

"That's depressing."

"These rooms are future ruins."

She gave me that familiar look that said, "Lighten up."

As we exited through the living room, past the piano, a glass display case, and Christmas tree, I thought to myself, *What will people think when I'm gone, and they sift through my ruins? I'm not sure I want to be defined by the artifacts I leave behind.*

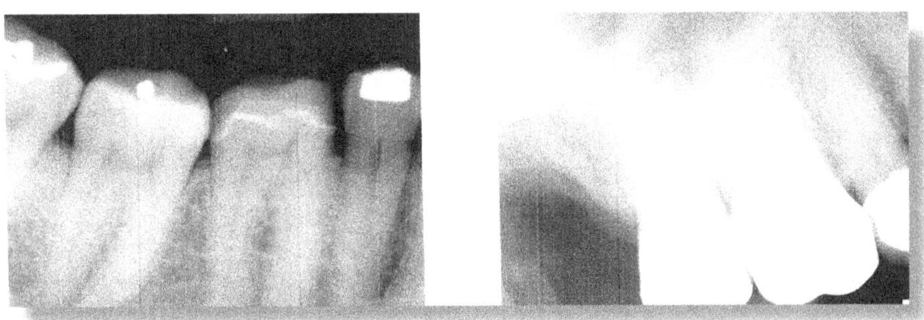

"Body Parts"

I thought he was going to yank out half my jaw.

"This one is a little tougher than usual," my dentist said casually, as he got a better grip.

My pulse was headed for Mars after he'd shot me up with epinephrine, even though I'd been assured for the third time by the receptionist, on the phone and in person, that it was noted in my chart and wouldn't happen. When I mentioned that my pulse was slightly elevated and my heart was doing backflips, she said the epinephrine would do that.

"But I have irregular heartbeats," I told her. "He wasn't supposed to give me epi."

"Let me check on that," she said and left the room.

I tried to slow things down with a little deep breathing like I'd heard from Dr. Weill. It wasn't happening.

"He didn't give you epi," she said, then checked my blood pressure and pulse. "It's not bad," she said. Of course, by then my heart was a wild mustang trying to kick its way out of my chest.

"Are you ready?" the dentist asked brightly as he bustled in.

"Ready as I'll ever be to have a body part removed," I replied.

"Sorry about the epinephrine," he confessed. "I saw you were allergic to penicillin but didn't look any further. I didn't see the note about no epinephrine."

Great, I thought, *next he'll be asking me which eye needed to be extracted.*

I closed my eyes, and he went to work. He yanked and twisted and pulled. I thought he'd have to leap onto the chair, straddling either side of me, feet braced against the back of the chair to get a better grip like I'd seen in all those Looney Tunes cartoons. Finally, I heard a soft tearing as the tooth reluctantly released from Tranquility Base.

"No wonder it was so tough," he said. "Three roots. That's unusual."

No, I thought, *it just didn't want to leave its home of 58 years.*

The assistant removed the hard rubber wedge from my mouth, placed a wad of gauze over the gaping wound, and asked me to bite down.

A little dazed, holding an instruction sheet and filled to overflowing with what to do if this or that happened, my wife drove us home and I began post-op. A succession of gauze pads and Advil. No alcohol and no real food. It bled most of the evening and through the night.

I remember my dad coming home after having two wisdom teeth pulled. I had never seen him in such pain. It made him seem so vulnerable, so mortal. He lay on the couch, sucked on gauze, and took pain pills all night. He and I had the same, brittle teeth. Heredity is a wonderful thing. I knew someday I'd be doing exactly what he was doing. And here I was.

Probably what bothered me the most, beyond the bleeding, the pain, and the inconvenience, was the loss of an old friend. There was now a hole in my mouth where a familiar, rough-edged contour had been. The decision to remove the tooth had come two years after I had chomped down on a raw oyster and a piece of shell cracked off the back part of my upper right wisdom tooth. I had lived with it, but it had finally gotten too sensitive to heat and cold and sweets. I had grown accustomed to seeking out the missing chunk of bone with my tongue. I knew it as well as I knew the other old friends populating my mouth. Like my chipped front tooth, the bridge, the crowns, the silver- and gold-filled cavities. Now the wisdom tooth was gone. And the dentist hadn't even offered to give it to me as a keepsake. Although that would probably have depressed me even more, like the thought of having my 12-year-old body's ruptured spleen pickled in a jar and resting on a closet shelf somewhere in the house.

I hate losing body parts. It's so disfiguring, so permanent and so mortal.

"Grampa Owl"

In honor of the Oakdale Rodeo.

He wore the best and rode the best. Silver buckles and silver saddles, snap-brim Stetson and polished boots. He survived two wives and married a third. He had three children and eight grandchildren. He was born, raised, and died a cowboy. His name was Alowishus Owen Wright. "Ace" to his friends. Grampa Owl to us kids since we couldn't pronounce his name.

He took us on cattle drives and to the stock yards. We rode horses and chased rats in his barns. He gave us cowboy boots and hats. He hoped that we, unlike his second son, our dad, would want to take up ridin' and ropin'. But, unlike Grampa Owl, Pater didn't have particularly fond memories of rising at the crack of dawn, loading the horses and tack, driving for hours, riding on hot asphalt in some small-town rodeo parade, returning home after dark, and having to bed down the cranky stock before bedding down himself. No, Grampa's dream just wasn't meant to be. We were city kids and that's the way it would remain.

Grampa Owl was dark-complected and spoke Spanish like a native. He denied it his entire life, but the odds were that he had Mexican blood. His mother, Julia, looked *mestizo*. His siblings – Uncle Pete, Aunt Aurora, and Aunt Rose – all looked Mexican.

He wasn't very affectionate, being he was a man of his era. The only time I ever saw him vulnerable was when he was in the hospital dying. He was hallucinating because his tobacco-scarred lungs were getting so much oxygen his brain was firing on all cylinders. It was driving him mad.

He and my dad were very different. Dad tried not to be like his old man. He was affectionate. He was available. He was kind. He was generous.

I would love to have known Grampa Owl as a contemporary. To know what he thought. What was important to him. What his dreams were. Why he did what he did. What he didn't do that he wanted to.

And where he got that hat.

"Strays"

Strays. We took them in. That's what we did. It's what we've always done. It's what we'll always do. Orphans, refugees, and loners. Animal and human.

They always found us. They always knew they could get a handout, or a helping hand. The hobos could smell what house to mark. Because we just couldn't say "no."

We didn't care what you'd done, were doing, planned to do. If you needed a friend or a home, you had one.

The reasons they came searching were as many and varied as they were. Parents who fought all the time or were divorced or too busy. Castaways just looking for safe harbor. Mothers and fathers who didn't get it, who didn't understand that music was just as important as math. Kids just looking for someone to listen, or spend a little time being asked about their day. Children who liked to laugh and enjoy life. Anyone who welcomed being left alone, not judged, and accepted for who they were, or dreamed of being.

Unfortunately, some of our strays got too comfortable. Once we removed the thorn from their paw, they never left. The good times, good food, and good company were just too good. They started getting a little fat. Some expected the acceptance to always be there, no matter what they did. So, they did some things they shouldn't have done. And suddenly they found the door was no longer open; that we did not forgive easily. Once that door was closed, it was very cold outside. Like F. Scott Fitzgerald, we didn't believe in second chances or second acts. If you burned us, or took us for granted, or didn't appreciate what we had to offer, you'd soon learn the meaning of long memory.

However, those who did know better, those who could read and respect us, never left. And never found any deeper, more loyal friends; nobody who would go to bat for them like we did.

And they are still part of the family.

Pizza image by Jacek Chabraszewski. © 123RF.com.

"Hob Nob"

It was a place, and it was what we did.

Hob Nob Pizza was a tiny pizza joint on McHenry Avenue near an irrigation canal. It's where we went every Friday in the fall after the football game. We'd go with our buddies or, if we were lucky, our girlfriends of the moment.

It was always so packed you could hardly move. Sardines in a can. And forget trying to order a pizza. You had to submarine your way through the crowd and past two wood accordion doors to get to the counter to order and then hope you could hear when they called your name to pick up your pizza.

The pizza wasn't great, but it was good enough on a cold, foggy Friday night. The cheese was always so damned hot it burned the roof of your mouth. But it was the place to be.

If the Davis High Spartans had won the night, everyone was in a good mood. If we had lost, there was usually a fight. Especially if someone from a rival high school showed up. Hob Nob was our pizza place. We had pissed in the parking lot to mark it.

Gary and I were able to find a place for his VW bug in the crammed lot out back. We pushed through the fogged-window backdoor and into the press of flesh. I immediately started looking for Jill. She had sat with her friends during the game and never looked once in my direction. I put on a brave front and ignored her, too, although I'd steal a glance from time-to-time.

We had started going out during the summer. We had gone stag to one of her girlfriend's parties and sort of gravitated to each other. By the time we were slow dancing to the Righteous Brothers, it was official. We then spent a lot of time together when our Hi-Y and Tri-Y groups collaborated on a float for the homecoming game. A Trojan horse molded around a small, black-and-white Nash Metropolitan owned by one of Jill's Tri-Y friends.

I was a bit possessive, jealous, and insecure, so we had hit a rough patch. She used to come by on weekends while I was doing yard work and other chores. I was pissed at her and had ignored her when she drove up. She left. And hadn't talked to me all week and had then snubbed me at the game.

Now, all I wanted to do was see her and smell her and get back to where we were. Unfortunately, there was an obstacle. His name was Stu. He was cool and he was class vice-president. Wide receiver and safety. I was a baseball guy, which wasn't nearly as groovy. Jill and Stu were talking. His back was to me, and she saw me as soon as I came in. So, she got really animated. And affectionate, leaning in to whisper something. I could feel my face turning red.

"Let's go," I said.

"I haven't ordered yet," Gary replied.

"I'll see you tomorrow."

I pushed through the crowd, out the back door, and headed up the canal bank toward home, certain it was over. By the time I reached Pike Park, I was ready to call her and apologize.

Ah, Friday night lights and fights. Football and pizza, young love, and hormones. Confusing and exciting, gut-wrenching and heartburning, comforting and reassuring. Some things mix better than others.

Wouldn't it be nice to be that much in love, again? All the time.

"Jackals"

"I'll shoot," Floyd cried, as he pointed the bow and arrow at Kevin's heart.

Tears streamed down Floyd's pink cheeks, flushed white. He always looked like that when he was angry and he was very angry now, as he straddled the wooden fence of his backyard, trying to protect his domain from the pack of neighborhood kids with nothing better to do on this Saturday morning than pick on the weird kid.

They were like jackals, bobbing and weaving and howling and looking for a weakness; taunting a wounded animal we could bring down and devour. They could smell his fear. They liked it.

Kevin's friends jumped up and down, made faces, howled, and threw rocks at Ted. Taunting and teasing him. Kevin wondered why they did it; wondered why he participated. We were social predators. It was our job to weed out the weak; ostracize those that didn't fit; didn't belong; couldn't cope.

We did it as adolescents, as teen-agers, as high schoolers, as adults. The judging never ended.

When Ted's mother came out the back door and yelled for him to stop, we scattered to the wind, hightailing it down the alley and back to the park where we would isolate our next victim.

"Canals"

We drive under the Iron Rainbow spanning I Street. Spelled out in metal and light bulbs are the words: "Water, Wealth, Contentment, Health." It's the motto of our city, although it lost to "Modesto, nobody gets our goat" when citizens were asked to come up with some slogan suggestions in 1911. The arch was completed in 1912 to promote the city by the Modesto Business Men's Association, which later became the Chamber of Commerce. The original slogan was intended to read "water wealth" as one phrase meaning an abundance of water and then "contentment" and "health," implying one led to the other. Somehow that connection got lost in translation.

As we cruise, my buddy's dad pulls on a tall Burgie beer he has stashed inside a small paper bag that looked like it had been designed just to disguise 16-ounce beers. We kids sip on the NEHI Orange Sodas he bought us. Gary's dad sings Tennessee Ernie Ford gospel songs in a decent baritone. Zeus, my buddy's loco Airedale, howls in harmony in the bed of the truck.

They say the two things that helped shape modern California are irrigated agriculture and the freeway. We cross over Highway 99 and head out Maze Boulevard along a canal.

Most cities in California have irrigation canals. Ours are part of the Modesto Irrigation District and carry water from rivers and reservoirs in the mountains to the Valley farmers, which is what made Modesto and the rest of the Central Valley the most productive agricultural area in the world. We grew up with canals, swam in them, fished them, threw shit in them, and tried to get to second base while parked on their dirt banks. We figured everybody had canals.

Gary's dad is a ditch tender for MID, whose motto once was: "Where the Land Owns the Water." His livelihood depends on flowing water. It's his job to make sure the La Grange dam continues to feed the canals that channel life-giving water to the farmlands of Stanislaus County. It was irrigation that turned the sky farmers of the county into year-round farmers. They transformed the Valley into a sea of wheat, the staff of life.

We pull off Maze, drawn by a collection of city police and Sheriff's county cruisers parked along the edge of the canal.

We get out, walk up to the edge of the canal, and look over the steeped dirt banks. A young girl, about 12, floats in the canal. Surrounded by water hyacinths, her amber hair is spread around her like Ophelia in her suicide dress. She's snagged in the grate that catches all the flotsam and jetsam people dump into the canal.

Staring at her billowing hair, I think of a field of wheat.

"The Peach"

Kevin and his friend, Phil, both ten years old, walked along Old Oakdale Road.

Back then, this part of Modesto was mostly peach orchards, grape vineyards, and flat, open fields. The side of the two-lane blacktop was dusty, and debris strewn. The two boys kicked up plumes of dust as they trailed Phil's grandmother and grandfather.

Babushka and *Dedushka*, as he called them, which was Russian for grandmother and grandfather, looked as if they'd just gotten off the boat from Kiev. Swaddled in dark, heavy, woolen clothes and thick shoes, she wearing a kerchief and he a peaked cap, they waddled along, heads down so as not to attract attention, which could be lethal for Jews in the *shtetl*.

Every so often, as they moved alongside the peach orchard, *Dedushka* would stop, stoop down, pick up a ripe peach, and tuck it into the voluminous pocket of his overcoat. He did this several times before they reached Scenic Drive, which was their route back into town and home.

"Why does he do that?" Kevin asked. "That's kind of icky."

"The peaches are good," Phil replied.

"Is he hungry?"

"Not now."

"So, what's the point?"

"It's an old habit and a hard one to break. In the old country, he never knew where his next meal was coming from. This kind of bounty was enjoyed only by the wealthy. There was no food just lying around on the ground. Especially something as exotic as a peach. For him, America really is the land of milk and honey. You and me, we take things for granted. Not him."

Kevin ran into the orchard, picked a particularly luscious peach, yanked it off the branch, caught up with *Dedushka*, and presented him with the golden fruit.

The old man looked up and his eyes crinkled in a smile. He took the peach, wrapped it in his clean, white handkerchief, and tucked it carefully in the inside pocket of his coat.

"Origami Haiku"

I had gone to the Haggin Museum in Stockton to see the landscape paintings of 19th Century artist, Albert Bierstadt. His luminous canvases captured Yosemite, the Delta, and the Central Valley.

One of the docents was an elderly Japanese American man. He didn't seem to want to be bothered by my questions. I decided to show myself around.

He caught up with me later in the basement, where they had recreated old Stockton. He gave me three origami birds – one each of red, white, and blue.

I hope someday he'll no longer need to apologize for the sins of his ancestral homeland.

"Rag Top"

Dedicated to Ray Bradbury, Mr. Electrico.

"Deep in winter they had looked for bits and pieces of summer and found it in furnace cellars or in bonfires on the edge of frozen skating ponds at night. Now, in summer, they went searching for some little bit, some piece of the forgotten winter."
– *Ray Bradbury, Dandelion Wine*

I'm a lizard. I love the heat. I could never live where it snows or rains all the time. My safe harbor is way out in Summer Country.

The Summer Solstice is my favorite day. The longest day of the year. The day the darkening begins, and we slide toward winter.

The gardenia is my favorite flower. It smells of summer and new beginnings. It's like a botanical time machine. I smell it and I'm there. Once more. Déjà vu all over again.

Summer means baseball and chlorinated swimming pools. Cool mornings, warm breezes, and late nights. It means camping and golfing, fresh-cut lawns, and BBQs. The Boardwalk, county fairs, home-made ice cream, and cruising.

It's the time of year when I want to smash the clock and burn the calendar.

It calls to mind *Dandelion Wine* by Ray Bradbury, and the magical summer of 12-year-old Douglas Spaulding, who realizes he's truly alive and learns many things about life. It's a book I read every summer to remind me. It is summer bottled and stoppered so you can taste any day by simply sipping a little dandelion wine.

When summer is here, all is right with the world.

Summer is the musty scent of old Boy Scout tents and sleeping bags in my friend's backyard, moving mattresses into the living room because there's no air circulating in the air condition-less bedrooms, and watching Johnny Carson until Dad comes home from his second job at the gas station.

Summer is itchy legs and backs from wrestling in the grass, black-bottomed feet and bee stings from never wearing shoes, and beet-red backs from too much sun.

Summer is fishing at Pine Crest Lake, freak rainstorms, and MoBand concerts in the park.

Summer is pesky mosquitos, Slip 'n Slide, fresh tomatoes, and cooling off in the canal.

Summer is the 4th of July parade, fireworks, and burning your bare feet on a smoldering sparkler.

Summer is Playland and Zero candy bars, girls in bikinis, and riding with the rag top down.

It is the perpetual summer of California where everyone is Peter Pan and no one ages. And every ending is a happy one.

I wish summer could last forever.

Belly tops, flip-flops
Lemonade, in the shade
Blue skies, hot guys,
Late nights, water fights,
Ice creams, sweet dreams,
Bathing suits, shooting hoops,
Party time, school's out,
Sleeping in, sneaking out
Summer's coming …
– Author Unknown

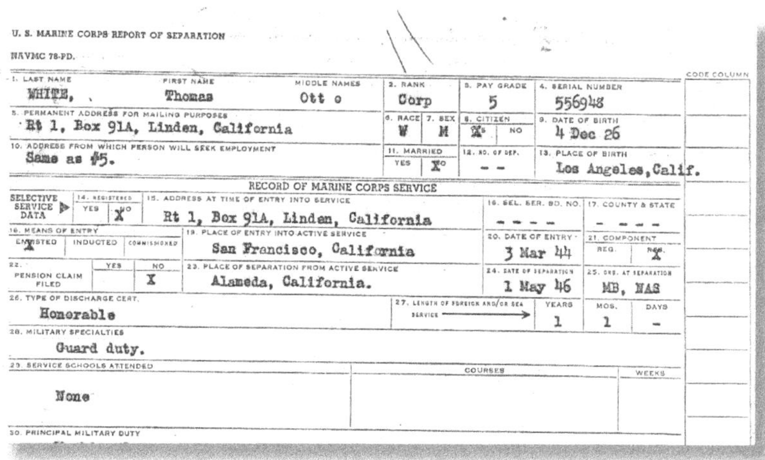

U. S. MARINE CORPS REPORT OF SEPARATION
NAVMC 78-PD.

1. LAST NAME	FIRST NAME	MIDDLE NAMES	2. RANK	3. PAY GRADE	4. SERIAL NUMBER	CODE COLUMN
WHITE,	Thomas	Ott o	Corp	5	556948	

5. PERMANENT ADDRESS FOR MAILING PURPOSES — Rt 1, Box 91A, Linden, California | 6. RACE W | 7. SEX M | 8. CITIZEN X | NO | 9. DATE OF BIRTH 4 Dec 26

10. ADDRESS FROM WHICH PERSON WILL SEEK EMPLOYMENT — Same as #5. | 11. MARRIED YES / X No | 12. NO. OF DEP. — — | 13. PLACE OF BIRTH Los Angeles, Calif.

RECORD OF MARINE CORPS SERVICE

SELECTIVE SERVICE DATA | 14. REGISTERED YES / X No | 15. ADDRESS AT TIME OF ENTRY INTO SERVICE Rt 1, Box 91A, Linden, California | 16. SEL. SER. BD. NO. — — — — | 17. COUNTY & STATE — — — —

18. MEANS OF ENTRY — ENLISTED X | INDUCTED | COMMISSIONED | 19. PLACE OF ENTRY INTO ACTIVE SERVICE San Francisco, California | 20. DATE OF ENTRY 3 Mar 44 | 21. COMPONENT REG. / RES. X

22. PENSION CLAIM FILED — YES / NO X | 23. PLACE OF SEPARATION FROM ACTIVE SERVICE Alameda, California. | 24. DATE OF SEPARATION 1 May 46 | 25. ORG. AT SEPARATION MB, NAS

26. TYPE OF DISCHARGE CERT. Honorable | 27. LENGTH OF FOREIGN AND/OR SEA SERVICE → | YEARS 1 | MOS. 1 | DAYS —

28. MILITARY SPECIALTIES — Guard duty.

29. SERVICE SCHOOLS ATTENDED — None | COURSES | WEEKS

30. PRINCIPAL MILITARY DUTY

"Report of Separation"

It's amazing how little we know about our parents. Their hopes and dreams at the various stages of their lives.

Once upon a time, my brother gave me a copy of my father's U.S. Marine Corps Report of Separation – Form NAVMC 78-PD. It was basically his discharge papers; a snapshot of the recruit just before he transitioned back into the real world. Nicely typed out on a manual typewriter with the requisite carbon paper copy.

As I scanned the document, I wondered who came up with the titles for each section and the required data for each.

It listed all the usual facts: name, address, date and place of birth, race, sex, citizenry, marriage status, rank, pay grade, and serial number. Where and when he entered and exited service, and type of discharge.

Then it got into more interesting territory.

His RECORD OF MARINE CORPS SERVICE held the first new information for me. His military specialty was "Guard duty." Did that mean that was what he volunteered for, what he was ordered to, what he was interested in, or what fell to him by default?

His principal military duty was "Machine Gun crueman," which I assumed was a misspelling of crewman. Or not. I remembered him telling us that's what he did, when he chose to talk about the service, which wasn't often. I wondered what kind of machine gun? How many men were in his "crue"? How many men did he kill? He would never say. We never pressed.

His EMPLOYMENT AND NON-SERVICE EDUCATIONAL DATA offered many additional surprises. His civilian occupation before he enlisted was "Student (H.S.)." He had enlisted at age 17-and-a-half before graduating from high school. His dad, Grampa Owl, accepted his diploma on graduation night. My dad had no secondary occupation listed. He had no last employer. He was a kid caught up in the patriotic fever infecting his country at the time. He and most of his buddies signed up to kill some Japs or Krauts or Wops. And that's what they did. After he'd been in the service for a short while, Dad called one of his buddies, who I was named after, and told him to forget the Marines and join the Navy, which his friend promptly did.

Under Trade Courses, nothing was listed. Under Courses of Greatest Interest was listed "Physical Ed." Did that mean he was a jock, or that phys ed came easily? Did he want to become a PE teacher? Why does one pick PE as a course of interest? I wished I could ask him.

PREFERENCES was the most revealing because it gave us a glimpse of his dreams. It was also the most frustrating because it raised so many questions. Under Preference for Additional Training, he listed "University." I knew he had always wanted to go to college under the G.I. Bill, but marriage and a family quickly derailed that and forced him to abandon his young boy ways. He always said he wanted to be an architect, which reminded me of George Bailey in *It's a Wonderful Life* and all those who lived "lives of quiet desperation," waiting for someday to arrive when they could do all those things they had daily dreamed of doing; all those "someday" things that many people never cross off their "to-do" list.

In his later years, he never missed going to a local stock car or NASCAR race. And each year, he meticulously charted with pen and paper the lap-by-lap progress of the Indy 500 on the back patio, while listening to the radio perched on top of the outdoor oven in the days before TV and ABC's *Wide World of Sports* coverage, which led me to wonder if he had dreams of being Parnelli Jones or A.J. Foyt or Bobby

Rahal.

Under Job Preference, my father listed "F.B.I." I had never known that or didn't recall knowing that. What was it about the FBI that had interested him? Had he been inspired by G-Men movies? By J. Edgar Hoover and Elliot Ness taking down Capone and Nitti? Guns, I doubt it. Forensics, probably not because he didn't like death. Investigation, perhaps, because it was a puzzle and a challenge. Maybe it was just exotic. Perhaps he was really just ready to do something as far removed as possible from Manteca and the Central Valley.

As I looked at the simple document, I wondered what happened to the young man sitting in a wooden chair beside the uniformed clerk who asked him the questions and meticulously typed in his responses? What turns in life changed what he wanted to be to what he finally became? I would never know because I never asked, and he was no longer here to ask. All that history died with him.

Such a loss. For us all.

"Have To"

"You have to apologize."

"No, I don't," Kevin replied. "He's the one that called me. He's the one that accused Sandra."

"He's your father."

"Sure as shit didn't act like it."

Gary never stopped trying to smooth things over; never gave up attempting to make things right. Sandra and I had been home for a short time after a very long Christmas day family celebration. The pot had boiled over at last. Sandra and Joan had finally had the showdown that had been brewing since Joan first met Dad. Sandra and Joan had never liked each other. They had been clawing to carve out their territory and their place in our family. And they had bumped hard into each other.

Apparently, Sandra had walked past Joan in the hallway of my sister Cheryl's house that morning and Joan thought Sandra had slighted her. Sandra apologized, explaining she meant no harm. Joan grudgingly accepted it. Then told Dad. The fact is, they both were guilty. It was such bullshit. I had had it with both of them and now Dad was suddenly stuck in the middle of it. Again. I know Joan had browbeat him into it. Guilt tripped him. Probably added a few tears to soften him up. Unfortunately, we were both that kind of guy, which meant I had to listen to my father rag on my wife and lecture me about how badly she treated his wife. And how disappointed he was in her – and me, by implication. I hated this.

It would take months to smooth things over so the two women could be in the same room together. They never really forgave each other. And I never forgave either of them for putting my father and me in that position and straining our relationship. They didn't care. They just wanted what was theirs.

That's one of many reasons why I've never been a big fan of "have to." Not then, not now, not next, not ever.

Have to make phone calls, have to do yard work, have to lose weight, have to do good, have to get along, have to drink water, have to apologize, have to have fun, have to take care of everybody. In my entire life, I've been paralyzed by "have to." It's always been there, hovering.

That's likely why I work for myself and probably why I never lasted too long in a full-time job. It's also why I've always had a hard time with classes, meetings, appointments, and commitments. I never liked having to be somewhere at a certain time on a pre-scheduled day to discuss specific things. Maybe it's oppositional, maybe it's dodging reality. But it's worked for me. So far.

I don't remember if I ever apologized to my father. I guess I didn't have to.

"The Maestro of Memories"

It's Thanksgiving morning in the Central Valley town of Modesto. A group of graying Baby Boomers play a football game in the rain.

Kevin limps off the field. He's tired and covered completely in mud and blood. Someone on the sidelines tosses him a can of cheap beer. He snags it and drains it. Kevin wears a baseball hat with the embroidered words: "Modesto JC." His torn football jersey reads: "The Mud Bowl – 30 Years of Refusing to Grow Up." He wears a canvas belt with two red football flags.

A second player appears at Kevin's side, throwing an arm over his shoulder. It's Kevin's younger brother, Tim Junior, also a combatant – but for the other team. He wears a UCLA baseball hat. His threadbare T-shirt features the image of a naked woman bent over and prepared to hike a football to a man with his hands cupped between her legs. The caption reads: "Play Naked." He wears a belt of yellow football flags.

The two brothers walk away from the action on the field toward a small knot of people huddled together against the rain and cold. A younger man and two younger women. From the striking resemblance, we can tell these are Kevin and Tim's brother and sisters.

As Kevin approaches, he thinks, *We were the closest of strangers. As good a family as some, probably better than most.*

The five siblings drift together into a ragged circle. William "Willy," the middle brother, wears an elaborate Indian war bonnet and a sweatshirt sporting the image of an Indian brave carrying a television set with a football game on the screen. The caption reads: "After the hunt, the men returned with the game."

Diane "Dee-Dee," the oldest sister, wears a child-made hat that somewhat resembles the Mayflower and a sweatshirt featuring the image of a turkey shaped like a football.

Cheryl "Cheri," the youngest sister and sibling, wears a Pilgrim woman's bonnet and a T-shirt that reads: "Tim Turkey Died for Your Sins."

A hand darts into view and flips Kevin's baseball cap off his head. The hand belongs to Gary Rawlings, Kevin's childhood (and oldest) friend. Gary wears an admiral's cocked hat with an arrow stuck through it Steve Martin-style. His sweatshirt proudly proclaims: "Runs with Scissors."

"We're serving Thanksgiving tomorrow," Cheryl reminds Kevin. "At the mission."

"What good will that do?" Kevin asks.

"I put you down for three o'clock," she says.

"Got a lot going on."

"You promised."

"There's clients waiting, and projects backed up."

"Typical," she says.

"Maybe next year," Kevin promises.

"Yeah, maybe next year," she replies

Kevin smiles, wraps his arm around his little sister's head, and rubs her scalp with his knuckles.

A female voice says: "Wants to make a difference – "

"But can't make a commitment," Gary finishes the sentence, then affectionately punches Kevin's shoulder.

The woman's voice belongs to Rory Jefferson, Kevin's wife. She wears fake Indian princess pigtails and a sweatshirt that reads: "Plays Well with Others." She joins the family circle, giving Kevin a wet, sloppy French kiss in his ear, which he promptly wipes away.

Timothy Woodworth, Senior – the patriarch of the family – walks up and joins the circle. He wears a snap-billed, sports car racing cap, a NASCAR sweatshirt, and a silk jacket with the name, "Owen," embroidered over the heart. Clinging to his arm is his wife, Joan. She wears a plastic, floral-print rain cap and a sweatshirt with an elaborately cross-stitched Berenstain bear.

"Got the bird in the oven," the elder Woodworth says, chuckling to himself.

"Not on the floor?" Gary asks.

"Kept both hands on the sucker this year," Tim Senior replies.

"I rationed his wine," Joan explains.

The five siblings are joined by the rest of their respective families. Tim's wife, Linda, and their two twenty-something sons, Jared and Travis, both covered in mud and sucking on beers, like their father and uncle. Willy's wife, Polly. Diane's two daughters, 16-year-old Carol and 12-year-old Kaitlyn. Cheryl's husband, Skip Laurenti, and their 14-year-old son, James, and 10-year-old daughter, Lucy.

Kevin herds them all into a half-moon for the annual Mud Bowl, Thanksgiving family portrait. They pose for the camera. In birth order.

The Mud Bowl was just one of many events Kevin was responsible for perpetuating. He was the organizer; the one who kept everyone together. Whether it was orchestrating the high school reunion every five years, annual family birthdays, the adult softball leagues, community projects, the family Christmas, or the elementary school softball game and BBQ, even the Bunko and pinochle tournaments, he was the maestro of memories; the raj of remembrances of things past; the town crier. And the documenter. Whether it was still photos, film or video, and words.

He was a pest about it. To family and friends, even casual acquaintances. He insisted on their being available to participate in the creation and capturing of moments. And if they chose not to, he got bent out of shape.

Of course, it was selfish. He wanted to see these people. He wanted to create those memories. And he became even more obnoxious as he aged because he knew those memories were precious. He knew that, as we grew older, we held onto our memories so dearly because we didn't know how many more we'd make.

"(You'll Never Love Her) As Much as I Do"

My dad was pissed. Again. I had yelled at Mom and now she was crying. She had said something, probably something innocent, like "clean your room" or "feed your dog," and it had pushed a button. We got into a yelling match, and I told her, "I hate you!" Which, of course, I didn't mean. It had just come out. Now she was in tears. She left the room, and I knew it would be trouble when Dad got home, so I made sure I was outside where there was room to move. He found me petting Ring, our dog, on the strip of dirt next to the patio.

"Apologize to your mother."

"It was all her fault."

"Because she asked you to do your chores?"

"I was going to."

"When?"

"Eventually."

I noticed that he had picked up a thin piece of wood which had fallen off the fence. When I was younger, he occasionally used a belt on us when we'd really screwed up. He'd tell us to go to our rooms and take our pants down, while he slid the leather belt out of the loops of his blue jeans. I hated that sound. A leathery slithering. He'd follow us into our room and tell us to bend over. All the while, we were crying and whimpering like we'd already been beaten. As he stood there, he'd almost always say, "This is going to hurt me more than you." I didn't believe it then, but I believed it later because he really hated spanking us. Sometimes, we gave him no choice. Sometimes, we backed him into a corner and there was no option. Of course, as soon as he raised the belt, we'd put both our bare hands behind us to protect our naked butts and our hands would take the beating. Today, he was carrying a wooden stick instead of a leather belt.

"Come here," he commanded.

"No," I replied.

"Don't make me come over there."

I'd heard that line a thousand times, too, but I wasn't budging. Then I made a dumb move. I ran. I figured I'd dash out the back gate and into the park. He was still young enough and could run pretty fast, but he was a smoker. Thanks to his cigarette lungs, I figured there was no way he could catch me. Evil thoughts, I know, but I was trapped. It was amazing how quickly those thoughts flashed through my head and helped decide for me. I took off. I bolted to my right toward freedom. Out of the corner of my eye, I saw him raise his arm and fire the stick at me like some ancient hunter. Like those hunters, he hit his mark. On the fly. He led me like a pro and the stick caught me in the left temple. I dropped like a rock and rolled a couple feet. When I stopped, I got to a knee and touched the side of my face. When I saw the trickle of blood, I started crying.

"I'm sorry, son. I didn't mean to," he said, as he rushed to my side and tried to help me up. By then, I was mad, too. I brushed his hand away, stood up, and walked a few feet away. He was shook up. I could tell, but I was enjoying it. *Serves him right*, I thought. I covered the bleeding with my hand, glared at him, and let him and his guilt twist in the wind.

"I hate you. And I hate her. I hate all of you. I wish I didn't have a mother," I hissed. "Or a father. I don't need any of you."

That was the wrong thing to say. His eyes narrowed.

"You're all the same," he replied. "Selfish. Your brothers and sisters are just like you. You take and take and expect more. It's probably our fault for spoiling you. You get what you want, what you came for, then you leave. And I have to pick up the pieces. I have to hold her hand and wipe away her tears when she cries herself to sleep wondering what she said wrong. Worrying that you still love her. That's what mothers do. They die a little each night because of their children. We fathers have to tell her it's all right. It doesn't mean anything. They still love you. The fact is, my boy, you – none of you – will ever love her as much as I do." He pointed a finger at me. "I don't ever want you to treat her that way again. You understand?"

I did, but I wasn't going to give him the satisfaction. I turned and ran. I kicked open the back gate and dashed into the park.

"Family Orbit"

"Everyone is a moon, and has a dark side which he never shows to anybody."
– Mark Twain

Kevin and Gary made candied walnuts at Gary's house. It was an eclectic and cluttered, but cozy, home. It overflowed with music, poetry, art, and books. Drawings by Gary and his grandkids and school kids covered the walls. His life's memorabilia were scattered throughout the house. A Christmas song by Jimmy Buffett played.

"You haven't made these in a while," Kevin said.

"Got too much crap from everyone."

"Last batch I had almost broke a tooth. Bit down on a shell."

"What'd you expect? I was drunk when I made them."

"Dad wants to invite Sally to Christmas."

"Whoa, no shit. Why?"

"Rory says he wants to tie up loose ends."

"He okay?"

"Why?"

"Only dying people do things like that."

"His heart's acting up again."

"It going to happen?"

"He wants me to talk to everyone."

"Big brother job."

"Don't know if they'll go along. I know Cheryl and Diane still think she's strange. Don't know about Willy. Timmy and I really haven't talked about it."

"We both know your family. You can't force them to do something they don't want to do."

"We all got that 'special' trait from mom."

"You think they should go along?"

"Guess I think we should all be in the same orbit."

"Like horses in harness."

"Yeah, sort of like that. When we aren't, I'm disappointed. It's always been that way."

"There's no changing them. You take them as they are, or not at all."

"Right now, it's not at all."

"Be careful. Your family, it's not like the weather. The days when you could take it for granted are long gone."

"It's funny. I want to see them, then I don't. I feel guilty when I don't try. We get along great when we're together. I miss it."

"The ebb-and-flow of family life. Every family has this little push and pull deal going on, this battle between wanting distance and wanting to be together. It's only human."

"Guess we're all in this together. No matter what."

"Always will be."

Kevin walked to a low bookcase. On top was an elementary school solar system model Gary had brought home from his class for the grandchildren to play with. Kevin turned the wheel that initiated the planetary orbits around the sun. It didn't move. He tried to turn it again. It still wouldn't move. He looked more closely at the mechanism. It seemed fine. He forced the wheel to turn. The railing that held the planets in place came unhinged. The planets all rattle-slid together. The sun slipped off its center perch, fell to the floor, and rolled away.

Photograph by Heather David.

"Santa Cruz"

Summer of '66. The Beach Boys propelled us over the hill to Santa Cruz. "Surfin' Safari" and "Surfin' U.S.A" filled our ears and minds. We were escaping the hot, dry, suffocating Valley. We were seeking the cool, clear, cleansing Pacific Ocean. And the blonded, bikinied surfer chicks.

Vanston drove his '55 Chevy with the two surfboards hanging ten for dear life, while Lanston snoozed, swaddled in his Block "D" jacket. Jim tail-gated in his '55 Chevy Nomad station wagon with its own boards. And Robert, with me riding shotgun and white-knuckling it, power-drifted the canary yellow '65 Mustang through the Santa Cruz mountains. Dave and the other Jim hunkered down in the back seat. Robert's customized stereo echoed off the redwooded canyons. He souped up sound systems the way our classmates tricked out cars.

We were the Valley Boys, the Sissified Surfers who skateboarded and belly-whomped the Curve because the ocean was a lifetime and lifestyle away. We wore Pendletons or striped surfer shirts, baggies, *Huarache* sandals, and our semi-long, bushy blonde hair with sweeping bangs resembling the Banzai Pipeline.

Robert had tucked pints of brandy and sloe gin in the Mustang's air cleaner so we wouldn't get busted if the CHP stopped us. For us high school graduates, the legal drinking age was still a few years away. We never got to toast the setting sun at the beach because some loser surfer punks spied the liberated bottles on the back seat floor and got to them first. We found the dead soldiers lying on the sand near the parking lot.

We cruised Beach Street and the Cocoanut Grove because that was where the action was. Vanston, Lanston, and Jim found the girls because they knew what to say and how to say it. Dave and the other Jim looked for trouble because it always came looking for them. Robert fiddled with his stereo because that's what he knew and how to do it. I walked alone along the beach because I didn't know any better and had no place else to go. The cool, salty air and screeching gulls were comforting.

Jan and Dean serenaded us as the sun sank into the ocean. And we headed home. Back to dusty reality.

"Someday"

So many ways to walk upon the earth
I trace my footsteps to the place of my birth
So what do you do with all your precious time
So many ways in which to reach for the sky
Someday, someday in a cloud of gray
I will, I'll make my great escape.
– Brett Dennen, "Someday"

I found Mr. Lowney sitting on a bench across from the entrance to a large, red canvas façade that read: "Mr. Electrico's Time Machine." He was staring at the open door.

"Hey, Mr. Lowney," I said.

He jumped, startled from his reverie.

"Oh, hey, Kevin. How was the arcade?"

"It was okay."

"Just okay?"

"Yeah, just okay. You been in yet?"

"Nope, getting up the courage."

"For what?"

"The unknown. No telling what will happen once I step inside that WABAC Machine. Not sure I want to know what's out there, you know. What's next and all that."

"Sherman and Mr. Peabody always change history and get in trouble when they time travel."

"That's what I'm kinda afraid of."

"Where do you want to go? Forward or back?"

"Old people always want to go back, son. There's nothing for them in the future."

"That's not true, Mr. Lowney. You've got a lot of road ahead of you."

"I wish, don't I wish."

"My dad always tells me to be careful what I wish for 'cause it might just come true. He usually says that when I say I wish my brother was dead."

"You should never wish that."

"I know that. Now. I guess I've been kind of mean to them over the years. Need to work on that."

"Good for you."

"Won't be easy. Hard to change old habits."

"I've got a few things left undone that I hope this machine can help me with. I left some things unfinished. A few of those 'someday' kind of things."

"Someday things?"

"Yep, like someday 'I'll learn how to play piano, or someday I'll write that book, or someday I'll get re-married.'"

"You going to learn how to play piano?"

"Something like that, Kevin. Something like that." He stood up. "Wish me luck."

"Good luck, Mr. Lowney."

"Save my seat?" he smiled.

"Sure thing."

"Yeah, what's that?"

He slowly shuffled toward the ticket booth, bought a ticket, turned around and held it up, then passed through the turnstiles, and entered the scarlet tent.

I guess I must've fallen asleep on the bench because I suddenly snapped awake. I looked around. It took a moment to remember where I was. I turned to gaze at the entrance. Just then, a young man wearing an old-timey Cubs cap and warm-up jacket stepped out of the doorway and walked toward me, smiling.

"I got what I wished for," the young man said.

"I'm sorry, sir, but – " I stammered.

"I'm playing for the Cubs tomorrow," he said. "I've got to get to Los Angeles. We're facing Drysdale."

"I don't understand," I yammered. "Who are you?"

"A man who's been given a second chance."

"What happened to Mr. Lowney? What'd you do with him?"

"Don't worry, he's fine."

"Where is he?"

"Gone home."

"I'm confused."

"Don't be. Just remember, son. Don't ever give up. On your dreams. On what makes you happy. On your family. On your friends. On anything that's important to you. Someone told me once, just like I'm telling you now, 'Life is too short to wake up angry, or with regrets. So, love the people who treat you right. Forget about the ones who don't. Believe things happen for a reason. Do one thing well, not a lot of things half-way. If you get a second chance, grab it with both hands. If it changes your life, let it. Nobody said life would be easy, they just promised it would be worth it.'"

I looked closer at the young man. He sort of looked like Mr. Lowney, especially the eyes.

"I'll miss you," I said.

"No regrets, slugger. No tears goodbye."

"Good luck."

"Luck is the residue of design, my boy. Old Branch Rickey said that." He touched the bill of his cap. "I've got a plane to catch." He took something out of his pocket, handed it to me, and walked into the night. It was Mr. Lowney's harmonica.

As I walked down the dusty aisles heading for the exit, I passed a wax museum housed in a lemon-yellow-colored tent. I saw effigies of Napoleon, Lincoln, Hitler, and Marilyn Monroe. Something odd caught the corner of my eye. I stepped closer and peered through the forest of waxen bodies. At the very back of the tent, a shriveled old woman was putting the finishing touches on a new display that looked disturbingly like the old Mr. Lowney. I blinked my eyes a couple of times and strained to see better in the dusky half-light. She placed an old fedora on the pomaded head of the dummy. She swiveled around and saw me. She motioned to someone at the front of the tent and the entrance flaps slapped shut.

Someday had finally come.

There ain't a lot that you can do in this town.
You drive down to the lake and then you turn back around.
You go to school and you learn to read and write.
So you can walk into the county bank and sign away your life.
Someday I'm finally gonna let go.
'Cause I know there's a better way.
And I wanna know what's over that rainbow.
I'm gonna get out of here someday.
– Steve Earle, "Someday"

Photograph by Brian Swander.

"The Bicyclist"

Dedicated to Swandez.

You never saw him without his bike. At the park, going to the bowling alley or pinball palace, on the streets, at the hospital, or back home to his mother's house alongside Pike Park. It's how he got from Point A to Point B. In a town of 30,000, it was practical. We all thought he was an odd duck. Of course, he couldn't drive because the cleft palate had made him mean and angry and anti-social. But he earned our grudging respect with his athleticism. He was a natural. He could have played baseball, football, or run track. Except for the cleft palate.

You never saw him without his bike. Carrying groceries home in the chrome basket, smoking a cigarette at a political rally in the park, going to a movie downtown, or back home to the house where his high school friend was raised and now lived and offered sanctuary. It's how he got around. In a town of 150,000, it was hard, but not impossible. We all thought he was strange. Of course, he couldn't drive because he had done too many drugs and had too many DUIs. But we put up with him because he was our classmate. Plus, he was funny. He could have done stand-up. Except for the addictions and the damage done.

You never saw him without his bike. Tipping his hat to the dogs and the whores on Ninth Street, delivering groceries to the seniors at Ralston Tower, handing out clean needles to the junkies in Tower Park, swaying to the beat of MoBand, or living in his tent down by the river. It was how he got from here to there and back again. In a town of over 200,000, it was dangerous riding a bike. Nobody paid attention. Nobody thought a bicyclist had the right of way. Nobody cared. We all thought he was crazy nuts. Of course, he couldn't drive because something had happened in the Iraqi desert when he was protecting our freedom. There was no "there" there anymore. But we accepted him because of his kindness. He could have been a saint. Except for the scars, visible and not.

You never saw him without his Raleigh. Bike that is. This collector of bicycle bells and ephemera. Rail-thin and dressed in turn-of-the-century garb, Dust Bowl attire, or artisan wear. His dog, Oro, sitting in the front basket. His portable desk and art supplies on the back rack, perhaps with a bottle of wine or beer. Capturing the world around him in sketches. Or a song. Or a wood sculpture. Or a set. Or a smile. Desperately, continuously trying to capture and contain time. And please those around him. Always ready with a smile or a story. Believing he was a man out of time. More suited to Guthrie and Dylan. It's been a long road from The Kitchen Sink until the end of the line. For this Renaissance Man. He never understood the power of love until the last days of his life.

In a world driven by expectations, they had none. They took things as they came and made the best of them. The sad and bad situations. They lived in the moment. Right here, right now.

And they were never disappointed.

"Fathers and Sons"

"When a father gives to his son, both laugh; when a son gives to his father, both cry."
– Jewish Proverb

It's complicated. Fathers and sons are. It's been said that it's up to the son to live up to his father's reputation or make up for his mistakes. Unfortunately, that's something we never can win. As sons, we are shaped by the tug of our father's expectations and the weight of his disappointments. We will always dwell in his shadow.

Fathers and sons have been rivals since forever. They have long competed for the respect of their community, the praise of their peers, and the love of their wife/mother. And, they've always had issues. Their conflict is as old as time, stretching back to BC and *The Bible*, before and beyond. Like Abraham and Isaac, or the Prodigal Son, the Good Book is full of stories about battles between men and their boys. As are myths, fables, and fiction, which tell more vivid tales of their clashes and struggles. As with Telemachus and Odysseus, Oedipus and Laius, the Hamlets, Geppetto and Pinocchio, George Bailey and Zuzu, Atticus Finch and Jem, Ozzie and Ricky, Mr. Cleaver and the Beaver. It's really nothing new. It's always been a kind of Greek tragedy. There were sometimes I hated my father, and other times I loved him. Sometimes I took his advice, other times I ignored it. Sometimes I wished he wasn't around, other times I feared my wish might come true.

For Baby Boomers who grew up when I did, it was up to the father to teach his son to be a man, to be tough in a cold, hard, unforgiving world. It was up to the mother to dress the wounds when that world kicked your butt. It was up to the father to provide qualified approval. It was up to the mother to provide unconditional love. It was up to the father to run alongside as you tried to ride your bike for the first time and shout encouragement as you did. It was up to the mother to stand on the sideline frightened you'd fall, and to wipe away the tears when you did. Fathers took charge. Mothers took care. Between them, with a little help from family and friends, community and society, a baby boy would grow up to be a man – a normal, productive, well-balanced, and committed member of society. In the case of Baby Boomer boys like me, that meant being self-assured, self-absorbed, and self-conscious about changing the world and making things right and filled with a sense of entitlement and great expectations for our own success.

Many believe a boy's struggles with his father make him a man. I never struggled with my father. That's because he, like many of the men of his generation and unlike the men of his father's generation, didn't feel the need to teach his children how to make it in a tough world. He believed his kids weren't going to live in the same world he had. It was bound to be better. My father and I didn't always agree. We didn't always see the world the same way. And we didn't always make the same choices. But, on the important issues – like family and the right thing to do; community and how you treated people and friends and taking care of each other; values and conformity for the common good and duty – we were as one.

Sports offered one of the best ways (sometimes the only way) a father could get close to his son. By listening to, reading about, or watching the game together; by teaching the game and perhaps coaching it; by keeping score and debating the strengths and weaknesses of your idols; the two of you could spend time alone together and learn to at least respect, certainly enjoy and appreciate, even like or love, one another.

Baseball was, in particular, a game that bound together fathers and sons. Like so many things, baseball was easy, and it was hard. It was gracious and clumsy, quirky and predictable, fair and foul, old and new, wild and controlled, relaxed and intense, fun and torture. Often it was all these things at once thanks to the expectations. That you enjoy it. That you were good enough. That you'd want to play it again. With him. That he'd have time for you now and you'd have time for him later. Baseball, in all its elegant and simple complexity, echoed the saga of fathers and sons, as well as the unbroken circle of life.

Baseball was the only sport for me. Probably because summer was my favorite season. Maybe because baseball was familiar. I understood it. I got it. And I could play it. There was something about the history and tradition, innocence and nostalgia, the symmetry and sense of fair play, the rite and ritual. Throwing, catching, hitting, running, and sliding all seemed so natural and effortless. It always made me think of a time when things seemed easier and better. I liked the fact that it was the player that scored, not the ball. That it included errors because we all made them. That it valued a keen eye, quick reflexes, and good judgment. That it was a team game. That it wasn't played against the clock. That, as writer Roger Angell once wrote, "Since baseball time is measured only in outs, all you have to do...is keep hitting, keep the rally alive, and you have defeated time. You remain young forever."

For me, baseball was the never-ending game. And it felt like home.

"The Portrait of Don Ho"

It was hot for September. The 40th Reunion of the Davis High Class of 1966 gathered at the Palms Restaurant in Modesto. It was the best attended of the previous seven gatherings. Perhaps because everyone was thinking this could very well be the last one.

There was one person I, as one of the organizers, was looking forward to seeing. He had been my good buddy, my baseball pal, my nature-exploring sidekick, my hell-raising accomplice before my real best friend moved into the neighborhood. I hadn't seen him since his father's company had moved the family to Milwaukee when we were in third grade.

As soon as he walked up to me, I knew who it was. It was in the eyes and the smile. And when he said, "Hello, Ringer," he clinched it by calling me by the nickname he had coined. And there was the chipped front tooth, which he got one summer when I pushed him down while playing grab-ass and he hit a slab of sheet metal lying on the bottom of an abandoned irrigation ditch. When asked why he never got it fixed, he would flash a toothy grin and explain, "It's part of my personality."

But he was now an old man. Grey-bearded, wrinkled, and a little stooped. Looking more like my grandfather than my peer. He was strangely familiar, and I felt mildly disoriented.

It's funny how our memory photograph of people is frozen forever in time, remaining unaltered until you see the real person in real time.

Sort of like the publicity photo of Don Ho.

"Poltergeist"

He limped toward the kitchen, half-asleep, eyes half-closed against the morning light. He opened the sun porch door he closed each night to keep the cats out of their bedroom. He saw the kitchen light blazing.

Not again, he thought, as he flexed his stiff right knee, another of the many body parts that were abandoning him in his sixtieth year.

He let the cats out, got the paper, and started the decaf coffee.

"Good morning, sweetie," his wife said, as she entered and grabbed his butt, all morning-person-chipper, and three years younger than him.

"You forgot to turn off this light again," he said.

"No, I didn't," she said, pouring herself a cup of coffee.

"I wonder if there's something wrong with the switch," he said, flipping it up and down.

"Have Mark check it."

"This is the third time this week. Last week Ethan's bedroom light was on a couple of times. A couple weeks ago, the TV was on."

"Must be the Poltergeist," she said, smiling.

"I swear that house in Montara had one. The property was on an Indian burial ground. It was haunted. How else would you explain – "

"The burner being on and the tea pot steaming," she said, reciting what she'd heard so many times before.

"It was a Poltergeist. What else could it be?"

"Short-term memory loss is an early sign of Alzheimer's," the doctor explained to her as she sat in his office, and he stared out the window.

"About Time"

"How did it get so late so soon? It's night before it's afternoon. December is here before it's June. My goodness how the time has flewn. How did it get so late so soon?"
– *Dr. Seuss*

It's about time. Slipping away. Being wasted. Running out. Standing still. Flying. Being lost. Filling, making, and killing it. Or, having enough of it.

We worry about it being the last time, or the last time around. It's always time to do this or that. We think about time zones, time outs, and real time; just in time or the nick of time or putting in time. We tell stories about once upon a time and share proverbs about a stitch in time. We fondly recall the first time and agonize over the only time. We try to take things one step at a time. We long for the time when time was on our side. Time and again, we talk about prime time, big time, me or my time, good time, nap time, in time, alone time, nighttime, hang time, Christmas time, every time, lost time, quiet time, any time, wintertime, sleepy time, strange time, short-time, part-time, all-time, the right and wrong time. We read *Time* Magazine or the *New York Times*, *Of Time and the River* or a *Brief History of Time*. We watch Time Warner or Lifetime. We nostalgically look back to the times of our life and hope we had the time of our life. We set our clocks to Greenwich Mean Time and Pacific Standard Time. From time to time, we ponder time management, which we'll get around to when we have time, and time travel which inevitably requires a time machine. We try to imagine what having time on our hands or the end of time really look like? We question if there is world enough and time. We sing "Time has come today," "Time after time," "Time in a bottle," and "By the time I get to Phoenix." We often don't have time to take our time. What came first, life or time? As one brainiac pointed out, if it weren't for time, everything would happen all at once at the same time. And, finally, there comes a time when we discover that Father Time waits for no one.

The older we get, the less there seems to be of it and the faster it goes. Something we thought took place two years ago was actually five. And we insist on rushing toward then without living in the now, this moment. Only to look back and wonder why we were in such a hurry for the arrival of tomorrow, when today will soon enough be gone to yesterday.

In the romantic comedy movie, *About Time*, a young man named Tim learns from his father that the men in their family have the ability to travel back in time. Not forward, just back, which provides our hero with the opportunity to change his past so he can have a better future. Near the end of the movie, Tim learns that his father has terminal cancer, which cannot be changed by time travel. When Tim reels back in time to visit his father the day before he is to be buried, his father counsels him to live each day twice. The first time to experience it in real time as it happens with all the stresses a "normal" person faces. And a second time, now knowing what to expect from the day, in order to savor each moment; embracing the day and enjoying it for exactly what it is. Like a good son, Tim follows his father's advice. But he soon realizes that it is a far, far better thing to live each day once and enjoy it as if it were his last.

It has been said that yesterday's the past, tomorrow's the future, but today's a gift and that's why it's called the present. As we start each New Year, this seems like an incredibly profound and valuable way to live each day.

"Time flies like an arrow; fruit flies like a banana."
– Groucho Marx

"The White Car"

I've known the white car longer and perhaps better than most of my family and friends and lovers. I bought it the year my nephew was born. He's now in college.

Mudbowl II and I have been together for more years than my first or second wife. I drove it home the day my mother died in her sleep. I drove it to see my father the day he died in the ICU. I drove it to see my best friend the day he died in the hospital. I drove it to my second wedding day. I've driven it through all four seasons. I've driven it drunk and sober. I've driven it when I was elated and depressed. I've driven it healthy and not. I've driven it when I worked for myself and for others. I've driven it to birthdays, holidays, vacations, Giants' games, reunions, as well as the homes of lovers, friends, and family.

It's always been discreet and non-judgmental. It's always gotten me from here to there and back again. No questions asked.

Yesterday, I passed it on to my stepson. I trust it will be there for him the way it's been there for me.

"What Are Little Boys Made Of?"

I was the oldest of five. They say firstborns learn to be resourceful, self-reliant, and tough. They demand a lot of themselves, and of others. They were organized and anxious. Always expected to set a good example. That was me, to a "T."

I had two younger brothers and two younger sisters. Timothy "Timmy" Owen Jr. was only fifteen months younger than me, so we were pretty close. William "Willy" Christopher, who was named after one of my dad's Marine buddies, was five years younger. Since he was the youngest boy, he got picked on a lot. He handled it pretty well. Diane "Dee-Dee" Jane was next in line. She looked a lot like Dad and was pretty easy-going, just like him. Cheryl "Cheri" Gayle was ten years younger than me and probably the most like me in personality. We were a family.

What are little boys made of, made of?
What are little boys made of?
'Snaps and snails, and puppy-dogs' tails;
And that's what little boys are made of.

What are little girls made of, made of?
What are little girls made of?
Sugar and spice, and all that's nice;
And that's what little girls are made of.
– Robert Southey, "What Are Little Boys Made Of?"

Each time I heard that nursery rhyme growing up, I realized it was true in so many ways, but it made me mad at girls. We were nice, too. We just enjoyed playing in the dirt more.

On any given day, little boys were also made of greed, envy, sloth, gluttony, wrath, pride, and lust. Pretty much some variation of all the seven deadly sins. We wanted what we wanted, and we wanted it now. We wanted what our friends had. We were lazy and would do as little as we possibly could, for as long as we could. We ate and drank anything and everything, any time we could. We got mad and held grudges forever. We believed the whole world revolved around us and were angry when it didn't. And we craved what we couldn't have.

My brothers and I were close because we rolled out of the womb one-two-three. I came out butt-first, but that's a story for a different time. Then Timmy. We did everything together, until Willy arrived. When he was old enough, he became the Third Musketeer. Any time you saw one of us, the other two were lurking nearby. We played sports, explored the neighborhood, victimized small creatures, threw rocks, played *Monopoly* and *Chutes and Ladders*, ran through mud puddles, dressed up for Halloween, wore hand-me-downs from older cousins, chased bees and butterflies, teased little girls and sisters, watched TV, played with matches, climbed trees, skinned knees, ran with scissors, caught polliwogs, nearly broke our necks on the Slip 'n Slide, played Cowboys and Indians and War, got brain freeze from ice cream cones, swam at Playland and in the canals, watched Saturday afternoon Westerns, rode horses at Grampa Owl's, gigged frogs with Dad, protected each other from older cousins and neighborhood bullies, sang songs, danced dances, and ate everything but peas, Brussels sprouts, and scalloped potatoes.

We were boys, and boys being boys, we naturally enjoyed the same things. We were inseparable, until someone got sick or hurt. Then you'd think we had lost an arm or leg. We shared everything. Disneyland, Christmas, family vacations, Easter, friends, bedrooms and bathrooms, school, summer, wagons and bicycles, sports, clothes, enemies, pets, chores, colds, heroes, and our hometown. It was a common experience and shared memory that only the three of us would have. Ever. Nobody could take it away. Ever. We were the only ones who could finish each other's stories and dream each other's dreams.

Until one of us was gone too soon.

"Only Time Would Tell"

The guy was named Stephan Marlow. He was an Air Force brat from Colorado, who had followed his older sister to UC Davis. He was scary bright, sarcastic, with a dark sense of humor. He was a poet and an admirer of the Russian decadent poets, thus his reason for being in the class. Sporting long hair, moustache, French cigarettes, Italian espresso, and Bohemian clothes, he carefully affected the garret scribe look. He reminded me of Eric Clapton in his Cream days. When it came to his world view, he was as radical as he looked.

He lived at the La Casa de Flores apartments off Russell, not far from my Vanguard apartment. His lady friend was named Jo, a petite, dark-haired beauty. He had a skittish Irish setter named Samba. I'd visit after class. We'd listen to music, classical or jazz. He'd smoke and drink espresso. I'd have a beer. If he wasn't working on a story, or playing acoustic guitar, he was doing pen-and-ink drawings of exotic places, people, or things. One, in particular, was the image of a Bedouin man sitting near a campfire, holding a hooded, hunting hawk.

He had once said to me, after a day when nothing went right, "People with great imagination have a hard time living in the real world."

Steph worked part-time at the Browsing Room in the library. It was an area where students could go to find quiet, listen to music, and read the daily paper, or latest magazines. Each seat had its own turntable. Steph checked out headphones and albums. You could sit for hours listening to the new albums he had ordered and carefully catalogued. Each weekday at noon, Steph would play a new album for whoever was in the room. It could be classical, jazz, rock, or world music. It was there I was first exposed to electronic music, such as the work of Walter Carlos and Morton Subotnick, whose albums *Silver Apples of the Moon* and *The Wild Bull* were mesmerizing, as was the cover artwork. Released by Nonesuch Records, the title for *Silver Apples* was inspired by the poem, "The Song of Wandering Aengus," by W.B. Yeats. The same poem had been responsible for the title of Ray Bradbury's collection of short stories, *The Golden Apples of the Sun*.

Steph had become friends with my professor, Rod Patterson. It was no surprise. They were similar. Inquisitive, bright, free thinkers. Men who could blend in with the Russian expatriates who lived in Paris during the time of Hemingway, Joyce, and Fitzgerald. Rod's home was in the country off Mace Boulevard. It was an older home with a concrete fence, both painted green, camouflaged by bushes and trees. It was open and airy. He and his wife, Marilyn, had a menagerie of animals. Steph and I would join them in the evenings and on weekends for coffee and conversation. We discussed Nixon, the war, the draft, Reagan, the university, People's Park, and their efforts to free Russian Jews from the Soviet Union. Rod was an innovator. He was continually looking for ways to improve and enhance learning and teaching.

The year of 1969 was filled with momentous events and memorable people – people I had known my entire life and people I had met this year. Family, friends, chance encounters, passing acquaintances. My family was a given. The friends weren't. I had become friends with Gary, Gover, Wally, Steph, and Rod for a variety of reasons as different as they were. Could that friendship sustain the changes that were bound to come? Would we go our own ways and become strangers? Only time would tell.

Excerpted from Brighter Day.

"Friday Night Lights"

In the spirit of James Joyce.

There was nothing like Friday night football, sitting in the stands on a fall night, while two sets of helmeted, padded, and cleated gladiators did battle for school pride. It was an opportunity to check out the cheerleaders, as well the rest of the girls at our school and the opposing school. It was a chance to show our school spirit and root for the home team. And try to stay out of fights. There were always hoods from our school and the rival school that were ready to pick on smaller kids and maybe each other, if they'd gotten enough liquid courage. Never a dull moment.

Kids, like schools of swarming fish, came together and separated in the autumn sunset, giggle-talking to one another, checking their hair and make-up while looking for the other, trying to find that special missing person and hoping they were looking for you, with waving banners of school spirit and widemouthed, laughing faces overwhelmed by everything drowned out by the uniformed pep band and short-skirted yell leaders under bright, white lights begging you to watch the game on the field instead of the game in the bleachers, but knowing they were a side-show not the main attraction as the announcer described the action and named names and the fans on the opposite side were a faint memory of hot dogs and See's suckers, cotton candy and cool evenings threatening rain, but you were packed so tight on hard, splintery, wooden benches that you were warm enough and hoped you wouldn't have to pee in a crowded bathroom before half-time when the drum major strutted onto the grassy field followed by a phalanx of uniforms, playing fight songs and Souza marches until the muddy combatants returned following a locker room pep talk, fired up and leaving it all on the dead brown field until the Zebra's gun sounded victory or defeat and everyone streamed away to their next rendezvous to do it all over again.

"The Happiness Machine"

For Ray Bradbury and my little brother.

"The happiest of people don't necessarily have the best of everything. They just make the most of everything they have."
– Author Unknown

"What is happiness?" my philosophy professor asked. "Money, health, a fancy car, a thin waistline, a meaningful career, doing for others? As the song says," he continued, "money can't buy you love. Or happiness. Is happiness getting what you want, or wanting what you've got?"

We, his students, who were the target of his question, sheepishly looked at each other, our hands, or the ceiling. None of us wanted to volunteer an answer – probably because we really didn't know, perhaps didn't care (it was the Sixties after all), and even more likely because it was our last class before Christmas break. *How could this bozo ask a question like that just before the clock would strike the hour and set us free to happily enjoy our holiday*? I asked myself, echoing his rhetorical.

For me, the answer was always elusive, always just out of reach. When, in fact, it was there the whole time, right in front of me, just waiting for me to see. And when I finally did, it was so obvious.

I always came home for the holidays. "I'll Be Home for Christmas" was my anthem. And I was there for every Thanksgiving and Easter and Summer. Some of my classmates never went home. I did. And I continued to as an adult. As long as Mom and Dad had a home, I had a place to go. Years later, my then college girlfriend and now my ex-wife would say that our real home was the home we were living in together, not my parent's home or her parent's home; not the "family" home. She was right, of course. But, for me, the stubborn and oppositional child, Modesto, and the house on the street next to Pike Park, were always home and would always be.

So, here I was, home from college for Christmas. All my siblings were there, with their significant others; some of whom stuck, some of whom didn't. Gary, my best friend and college roommate, was there with his girlfriend and six-pack of Bud. There were a couple other high school buddies because this was the gathering place. The family room was cozy-warm and smelled of woodsmoke and chocolate chip cookies; cinnamon and pine; beer and cigarettes. Bing Crosby crooned through the ceiling speakers. The eggnog and ribboned hard candy tasted so very sweet. The blanket draped, Naugahyded couch felt soft and familiar. The colored lights glowed on the tree. The mistletoe hung with care. I was in safe harbor, and it was good.

I stepped out the family room door onto the small concrete backyard patio to get a breath of fresh air and gaze at the witnessing moon. I turned to look back on the scene inside. The large, segmented, rectangular picture window framed everyone and everything. And there it was. All of it. And it was working. In all its glory. The Happiness Machine. It had been around and running from day one; not always well, but still in operation. Sometimes, it needed tinkering and adjusting and oiling. When it was in tune, it was comforting and reassuring in its perpetual motion. It was something you could count on. Always, and mostly, when it mattered.

For me, happiness would always be family, friends, and home; and my heart would always be there. I realized then, and still believe now, that it wasn't about getting what you want, but wanting what you've got. It wasn't about having what you want but wanting what you have.

I felt sorry for those who didn't.

"Things turn out best for the people who make the best of the way things turn out."
Art Linkletter, Radio/TV Personality and Author

"Think of Me"

"I'm not dead yet," he said, echoing the line from *Monty Python's Life of Brian*, one of our favorite movies. Then he smiled that half-assed, shit-eating, ball-busting half-grin of his. I must have had that look again. The look that hinted at the reality no one wanted to face. The look that said he'd be gone soon.

"I know that," I replied.

"You're acting like I am."

"I'm sorry."

The Band was playing "The Weight" in the background. *Jeopardy* was silent on the TV. I was wondering what this world would be like without this goofy guy I'd known since third grade.

"We should go out on tour," he continued. "Call it the 'Not Dead Yet Tour.' Invite the Stones, Van Morrison, Rod Stewart, McCartney, Neil Young, and whoever in The Dead isn't dead. All those old farts who aren't dead yet but should be."

I was reading through the diary he'd kept while we traveled through Europe together just after we graduated from UC Davis. He was looking through the photographs we'd taken on that trip. He had gone to see the world one last time before starting work. I had gone to see the world, too, because there was a good chance my next tour would be in Vietnam. I might not be coming back.

This particular afternoon, we were trying to cover as much territory as we could in the time we weren't sure we had left.

He tried to play flute along with the music but didn't have enough breath. He tried to eat but had no appetite. He tried to recite a poem but couldn't.

"I'd like you to read this at my funeral," he said

"You're not dead yet," I paid him back and smiled.

"Just read it, asshole."

Much too soon after that conversation, a fellow poet and friend read this poem at his funeral because I couldn't.

Work like me in gratitude
Glad to be alive
Then at the end of all of this
Sing and laugh and cry

Wrap me up, a gift of God
Lay me in the earth
I've known my life as dark and light
Half of what it's worth

Play like me inspired by
The songs that are your own
Some may try to silence you
But don't stop until you're done
– George A. Rogers, "Think of Me"

Think of me – share the smile
The one you can't forget
The smile that lasts past midnight
And know we're not there yet

Rest like me in fullness
Beyond knowledge, beyond fate
Trust the love that's everywhere
Rest now, sure in faith

Think of me from time to time
When you hear a song
You will know that love's not lost
And I'm not really gone.

"The Loner"

For Borges and the Mudcat.

"We're all alone out there. And tomorrow we're going out there again."
– *The Big Chill*

Weary, he wanders the crucified landscape. Alone.

Exotic in his moustache and goatee, floppy straw hat and shoulder-length hair. A haggard, scimitar-faced Bedouin, falcon at hand, red hound curled at his feet. Sipping espresso, smoking Gauloises, and peeling blood oranges. Lean as the flank of a hungry jaguar, his jaded smile is wreathed in rings of smoke.

The artist, the aesthete, the author. He, of the tortured soul, speaks in parables, metaphors, and similes; labyrinths, webs, and mazes. Spinning and spiraling crystal blue notes into the air.

He seeks solace in vast geographies of ink and infinite constellations of words, not a lover's arms. A slave to his incomplete and viciously tyrannical visions, his fountain pen relentlessly spins tales in endless, black-bound notebooks. With gentle cruelty, he mocks himself, his world, and the others.

He dwells in prosaic imagined places named Aleph, Ituzaingo, and Timbuktu. And in that silver Valley of the moon where wasted youth and squandered dreams abide. Deep into the night, he conjures images of Lorca and Aranjuez, Borges and Buenos Aires, Balmont and Petersburg, Neruda and Machu Picchu.

Cloaked in his anonymity, he is at once the dreamer and the dreamed. He doesn't need anybody. Or want anything. He is splendid in his enigmatic isolation.

Through the years, he has traced shadows of peoples, places, and things in a vain attempt to define, manipulate, and control his world and, ultimately, delay the patient insanity. One day, he discovers that the infinite labyrinth of lines he has been zealously pursuing traces the contours of his own face. At last, he understands there is not a single thing in this existence that time does not wash away, or memory alter. Beaten down by the common monotony of the day-to-day, he contemplates falling on the open blade of now.

One day, he disappears into his imagination. Never to return.

Know when you see him,
Nothing can free him.
Step aside, open wide,
It's the loner.
– Neil Young, "The Loner"

"Aunt Sis"

There are many things I remember about my Aunt Sis.

Watching her play softball.

Playing "Three Flies Up" in Pike's Park behind our house when the family visited.

Using her glove during a Little League game and catching a ball that dropped out of my teammate's glove while she and my parents watched.

Going to the beach in San Diego.

Eating tacos.

Hearing Uncle Joe and Aunt Sis laugh. Heartily.

Observing, and only later truly appreciating, their love and zest for life.

And, most of all, recognizing how very much she loved and protected her little brother.

A lot of people said we looked alike. I think we did. I think we acted alike, too.

There will never be another quite like her.

"Lágrimas"

"There is a sacredness in tears. They are not a mark of weakness, but of power. They speak more eloquently than ten thousand tongues. They are the messengers of overwhelming grief, of deep contrition and of unspeakable love."
– *Washington Irving*

We have used Tear Catchers since before Christ's time to collect our tears, marking life's rites of passage.

In Psalm 56:8 of the Old Testament, David prays to God, "Thou tellest my wanderings, put thou my tears in Thy bottle; are they not in Thy Book?" Mourners in Roman times filled small glass bottles or cups with tears and placed them in burial tombs. In the Victorian Era, mourners collected their tears in bottles with special stoppers that allowed the tears to evaporate. Once the tears disappeared, the mourning was over. During the American Civil War, women cried into tear bottles and saved them until their men returned from war.

Today, we give them and use them at times of loss and bereavement, weddings, births, graduations, anniversaries, and moments of sorrow and joy.

Through the years, I have collected tears for my mother, my father, my best friend, my little brother, and college buddy, as well as for lost loves and lost dreams.

The older we grow, the more bottles there are to fill.

Here I sit on Buttermilk Hill
Who can blame me, cryin' my fill?
And ev'ry tear would turn a mill,
Johnny has gone for a soldier.
– Traditional, "Buttermilk Hill (Johnny Has Gone for a Soldier)"

"The Christmas Gypsy"

"The mind is a strange and funny thing. In the summer it longs for winter, and in the winter, it longs for summer."
– Swami Muktananda

Kevin and Gary cruise Christmas Tree Lane in Gary's red, Nash Rambler. The car is festooned with Christmas lights. Two real antlers and a fake, red nose protrude from the front grill. This time of year, Gary's car is known as "Rudy."

Houses on both sides of the street are obscenely decorated for the holidays. Kevin wears his own set of felt antlers. Gary wears a raggedy, moth-eaten Santa hat.

"We've been at this a very long time," Gary points out.

"In junior high, the parents drove. We sat in back," Kevin says.

"And drank Nehi orange sodas."

"In high school, we drove."

"And drank beer."

"In college, our girlfriends drove."

"And we smoked dope."

"After college, our wives drove."

"And we snorted coke."

"Then our kids drove, and we sat in back."

"And drank Maalox."

"Now it's just you and me. No wives, no kids."

Gary toasts him with a Nehi orange soda and sings, "Will the Circle Be Unbroken?"

They pass a long line of cars traveling in the opposite direction, filled with kids and their parents, high school kids with their dates, old people and their caretakers, all pointing at the amazing display.

Kevin blows on his hands. "Damn, it's cold. I'm ready for summer."

"You're amazing. You're just never happy with what you've got. With the way things are."

"Maybe next year we'll just skip Christmas and go to Mexico."

"That's what I mean. When you're safe at home, you wish you were having an adventure. When you're having an adventure, you wish you were safe at home. You always want to be somewhere else. It's like Christmas in California. All the spoiled children think they're supposed to be having a good time, and they imagine everybody else is having a better time."

"Just saying I'm not a winter person, that's all."

"No, you're a Christmas gypsy."

"Pappy and the Duke"

That last Sunday in May 1969, KTXL Channel 40 in Sacramento ran a movie marathon in honor of the 62nd birthday of actor, John "Duke" Wayne, who was born May 26th, 1907. Most of the films they chose were ones he had done with director John Ford, including *Stagecoach*, *Fort Apache*, *3 Godfathers*, *The Quiet Man*, and *The Searchers*. They also showed pictures he had done without Ford, which included *The Alamo* and *The Green Berets*.

Like music, movies were a touchstone for me. They were a time machine. A way to conjure up memories. A way to re-experience past moments in my life. Watching a movie transported me back to who, what, where, when, or why I was. Good and bad, I was lost in the movie and the moment relived.

Joining me for this celluloid endurance run were two other John Wayne fans. Gover, Wally, and I hunkered down on the couch in our apartment. We had the place to ourselves, with plenty of junk food, beer, and a pint of Jim Beam.

"I'm so hungry I'm farting fresh air," Gover proclaimed.

"Keep it to yourself," Wally answered.

I passed him the tin of smoked oysters.

As soon as we saw the Duke as the Ringo Kid in *Stagecoach*, holding his saddle, cocking his rifle, and halting the stage, Monument Valley stretching out behind him, we cheered and took a slug.

I had long admired the work of John Ford the director. I had long enjoyed John Wayne the actor, but not John Wayne the politician, who had become Orange County conservative. I would learn one day that Wayne's ultra-patriotism may have been the result of him not serving in World War II, due to his being older than draft age, his work commitments and schedule, as well as being a husband with young children. It was a fact that director Ford, who did serve, never let him forget. Wayne would later admit that America thrived on change; that as laws, ideologies, and mores changed, so did society. And that was a good thing. Over the years, I may have judged Wayne too harshly. He may have been more of a pacifist and realist than what I, or his public, saw.

The second film was *Fort Apache*, another western epic shot in Monument Valley and released in 1948, the year I was born. It was the first in Ford's "cavalry trilogy" that included *She Wore a Yellow Ribbon* and *Rio Grande*. As the end credits rolled, I made the mistake of saying what I was thinking.

"Reminds me of Vietnam," I said.

"Say what?" Wally replied.

"Henry Fonda's Lt. Col Thursday underestimated his enemy. Wayne's Captain York did not. He knew they couldn't win."

"We can win in Vietnam," Wally countered.

"Not if we don't know better who we're fighting and don't adapt better to the terrain we're fighting in."

"You're being too damned introspective," Gover added, always the mediator.

"York spoke up," I went on. "He told the truth. Thursday didn't listen and paid for it."

"He did his duty," Wally said. "He put his country first. His honor second. His self last."

"Blind loyalty like that is crazy. Doing his duty led to his death and the death of all his men."

"He followed orders."

"His by-the-book stubbornness was lethal."

"He obeyed the chain of command."

"It's okay to break that chain and admit when you're wrong."

"He died in service to his country."

"I'm sure that was a great comfort to his wife and daughter."

Gover broke into our debate and said, "I read something, or was told by someone, I don't know where or who, that the story and his character were based on Little Big Horn and Custer."

"Another man who didn't respect and fear the skill of the 'savages' he was ordered to exterminate," I said.

The movies Ford and Wayne made alone and together were also about what they believed it meant to be a man. I had seen nearly all their collaborations, as well as most of the Duke's films. It seemed like those old black and white war horses were playing all the time on Saturday afternoons on one of the local stations.

Next up was *3 Godfathers*. Also released in my birth year, it was a beautifully shot technicolor film that echoed the story of the birth of Christ and the Three Wise Men. A story of three tough, hardened outlaws trying to protect a mother and her child; three men protecting the weak and defenseless, regardless of the personal risk; three men trying to do the right thing.

"He didn't give up on his buddies," Wally said. "He was loyal to the end."

"He always was. In the movies, or real life," I said.

"They trusted him. And he trusted them," Wally said

"He kept his word," Gover said.

"Even though he could've been arrested, or hanged," I said.

"There's some things a man can't run away from," Wally added. I knew he was talking about more than the movie.

After that was *The Quiet Man*, Ford's homage to his Irish heritage. A western that wasn't a western. A talented cast, including Ward Bond, who was a regular in Ford's acting company.

"Hubba, Hubba," I said, as Wayne dragged Maureen O'Hara across the emerald fields of Inisfree.

"Ding, ding," Gover chanted.

"Chop, chop," Wally added.

"Camp Ti-Wa-Ya-Ee, great!" Gover finished.

"I was talking about Maureen O'Hara, not your Boy Scout camp," I said.

"She was a babe," Wally admitted.

"Ford liked casting strong women," I said.

"And the Duke liked starring with them," Gover said.

"But he never got the girl," Wally said.

"That wasn't the point," I replied.

"He wouldn't fight the brother," Gover observed.

"Stayed true to who he was," Wally added.

"You don't have to resort to violence to win," I said.

"When he had to, when he had no choice, he did," Wally said. "And won her brother's and the town's respect."

"And the girl. This time," Gover said.

"I understand being strong when it's necessary, but I prefer being kind."

"Wuss," Wally replied.

"Kiss my butt," I said.

"Looks like your face," Gover said. We lifted our cans in toast to the predictably typical exchange and drank.

"Faint heart never won the field," Wally said, surprising me with the mangled English proverb.

"But he sometimes won fair lady," I said, correctly finishing the proverb.

Following that was my favorite movie of theirs – *The Searchers*. The characters Ford created, and Wayne portrayed, were all about the rugged individualist. In many of their movies, we saw the delicate balance between the individual and the community, wilderness and wildness versus hearth and home.

Wayne's character, Ethan Edwards, was the ultimate loner. A man bent on revenge. The last image of the picture was a memorable one. Wayne standing alone in the desert framed by the doorway of the homestead; a man destined to wander the outlands beyond civilization.

"Damn, that was brutal," I said.

"The Duke can act," Gover added.

"He's a different type of hero in this one," I said.

"A lot harder," Wally replied. "More real."

"Reminds me of a character he played in *Red River*, one of his earlier films," I said.

"How come they're not showing that?" Gover asked.

"It was done by a different director," I replied. "Howard Hawks."

"He couldn't be tamed," Wally added.

"He would always be an outsider," I said.

"An avenging angel," Wally observed.

"He was willing to kill his niece, Debbie, to save her," I said.

"But he didn't. He took her home."

"Even though he was an honorable man, he was a racist," I said.

"They killed his family," Wally countered. "And Martha, his sister-in-law. The woman he loved. No wonder he hated the Comanch."

"The white man killed the sons of Scar, the warrior who captured Debbie," I replied. "No wonder he hated the white man."

"Eye for an eye," Wally said.

"Some reviewers thought Debbie was Martha's daughter, which is why he was so determined to find her," I said.

"Family is all that matters. It's everything," Wally said. "I'd do the same thing."

"Kill her?" I asked.

"Hell no," Wally answered. "Take her back."

"That act saved him," I said. "He found redemption."

"He couldn't save everyone," Wally added.

"He tried," Gover said.

"This time Ford showed both sides in good and bad light."

"It's complicated," Wally observed. "We fear what we don't know or understand."

"He walked away," Gover said. "From family. From civilization."

"He became the loner," I said.

Then came *The Alamo*. A patriotic epic that nearly bankrupted and killed the Duke. He produced, directed, and starred in it. It was a huge production. As a result, his smoking habit skyrocketed. Even John Ford couldn't save this one, although he tried, without being asked, which created a nearly irreconcilable rift between the two men.

"That was bad," I said. "Too jingoistic for me."

"Those colors don't run," Walt replied. "They were badly outmanned, and they failed, but they tried."

"Bad propaganda," I answered. "He probably assumed this movie could get the whole country to rally around the flag."

"His answer to the protestors who are running down our country, hoss," Wally said.

"Thanks, Merle," I replied.

"No different than our fight for independence," he answered.

"It was Mexico's land. We wanted it."

"Manifold destiny," Gover said, chuckling.

"Every fight we've ever been in has been a fight to protect American values," Walt argued. "It's about freedom and a person's right to make their own decisions."

"Study your history," was all I said.

"Up your chocolate speedway," Wally replied and smiled.

"Sure wasn't the story Disney told," I said.

"Sure wasn't Fess Parker," Gover added.

"He was prepared and willing to kill, even die," Wally answered. "Most men aren't. He was."

The last, and certainly the least, was *The Green Berets*. It was even more patriotic than *The Alamo*, which didn't seem possible. It was the Duke's attempt to convince America to remain in Vietnam until we had won. We broke out the Jim Beam for this one.

"Didn't we see this at the Starlight Drive-in?" I asked Gover.

"We did," he answered.

"Didn't we drink Jim Beam just like the Duke?"

"We did."

"Didn't we do some damage to our bodies?"

"We did."

"Didn't you and Gant do some damage to our apartment doing the same thing while watching the same movie last February?"

"I know nothing," he replied, imitating Sergeant Schultz's line from the TV show, *Hogan's Heroes*."

"It's sad," I said.

"What's that?" Wally asked.

"The Duke let his politics destroy his craft."

"Could say the same about Peter Fonda," Wally countered.

"Not in the same class," I replied.

"Big John is balancing out the lefties in Hollywood," Wally said.

"Too heavy-handed."

"Sometimes that's what it takes."

"It's too black and white."

"No, it's color," Gover said.

"Too cut and dried. Too simplistic. Our goal is noble. Their's isn't. We're squeaky clean. They're slime balls."

"He was trying to tell the rest of the story."

"Like Leni Riefenstahl," I said.

"Who?" Gover asked.

"She did films for Hitler."

"Not the same," Wally answered.

"Anyone who's been to war isn't ready to start one," I countered. "That's how my dad felt."

"*Semper fi*," Wally said.

"It's how he would have felt about Vietnam, too. It's not World War II. We're the oppressors. They're dying for their freedom. For their country. For what they believe in. We can't say that. This movie and this war are both about pride and glory. We can't win. We need to admit it and admit we're wrong. That's the right thing to do."

"There's nothing wrong with pride," Wally said.

"*Hubris* has been the downfall of many men better than you or me or the Duke, and countries greater than ours," I argued.

"I'll always be better than you," Gover said.

"Me, too," Wally added.

With that, they both jumped on top of me, kicking off the wrestling match that generally seemed to end these get-togethers.

Excerpted from Brighter Day.

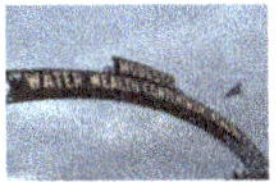

"Light My Fire"

For the music and the MAMAs.

"Light My Fire." The winter of '67. The flip side of the awakening. The Doors playing at a roller-skating rink in Modesto. Not wanting to be there on a dark Central Valley night. The opening act was a good friend's band, the Kitchen Sink. Five teen wanna-bes with a good sound.

On the inside, Jim Morrison was smoking and sultry. On the outside, two gangs of hoods were beating the hell out of each other.

I thought about the old and the new; one living, one dying, in 4/4 time.

"Magic Mountain"

"Goodbye and Hello." The summer of '67. Tim Buckley backed by Carter C.C. Collins on congas and percussion. KFRC Fantasy Fair and Magic Mountain Music Festival at Mt. Tamalpais in Marin. A benefit for the Hunters Point Child Care Center. The first "official" outdoor rock concert. The inaugural event of "The Summer of Love."

For two bucks, 15,000 of us witnessed the Byrds, the Jefferson Airplane, Sons of Champlin, Captain Beefheart, and Merry-Go-Round. Hell's Angels on hogs directed traffic. "Trans-Love Buslines" shuttled folks from the parking lot to the open-air amphitheater. We knew we could change the world with words like peace and freedom.

I wondered if I should wear flowers in my thinning hair.

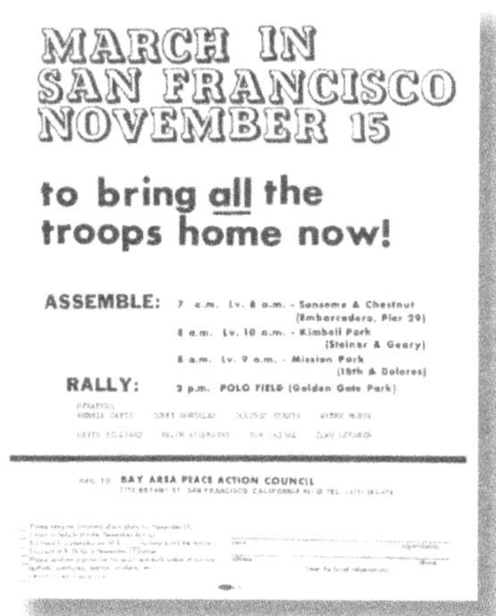

"Long Time Gone"

"Long Time Gone." November 1969. A foggy San Francisco day. The Polo Grounds at Golden Gate Park. The Moratorium to End the War in Vietnam. My first taste of revolution, of defiance, of togetherness. 125,000 people looking for a reason to believe. Rock 'n roll riding point. CS&N wearing those furry coats. Stills pounding out "For What It's Worth." They wandered among the people after their set.

I remember walking by them and thinking how short they were.

"Kid Guitar"

"Wanted: Blonde bass player with big tits." The sign on the broken-down Ford Econovan parked near downtown Modesto is scripted in ransom note lettering.

Kid Guitar rocks on his heels next to a tattered lawn chair, playing his Les Paul Cherry Sunburst guitar. Some decent blues licks croak from the tiny Pignose amp resting on the cracked concrete. He is short, portly, with long hair and a Rasputin beard. He looks like the bastard offspring of Tolkien's Bilbo Baggins and ZZ Top's Billy Gibbons. He wears a red nylon mesh baseball cap with the word "Modesto" stenciled on the front. Blue jeans, sneakers, and beneath the plaid work shirt, his raggedy-ass T-shirt bears the image of his god, Eric Clapton.

"He can still play," my best friend says as we stand there, watching the Kid pick and grin.

"He's not bad," my youngest brother says.

"He's almost as good as you," I say.

"Some days he's better," he replies.

"What happened?" I ask.

"I liked the home cooking."

Funny thing about success. It takes some serious ambition. And a lot of luck. Those who make it, want it. They're in the right place at the right time. But it also takes hard work. The great sage, Yogi Berra, said it best: "Success is one percent inspiration and 99% perspiration." Or was it, "95% of this game is half mental." Or maybe, "If you don't know where you're going, you'll end up someplace else." Yogi was never clear, even when he was lucid.

My brother was a talented musician. An absolutely killer guitar player. He never got the recognition he deserved. I considered myself a pretty good writer. I never got anything published. I always wondered why. On both our accounts.

Later that day at home, the smell of chicken BBQed in Woody's, my dad's favorite sauce, fills the summer air.

"Dinner's ready," my wife says.

Born under a bad sign.
I've been down since I began to crawl.
If it wasn't for bad luck,
I wouldn't have no luck.
If it wasn't for real bad luck,
I wouldn't have no luck at all.
– William Bell, Booker T. Jones, Jr., "Born Under a Bad Sign"

Postscript: I wrote this story long before my brother passed away. Before he recorded his solo CD. Before I published my first book. We both proved me wrong. You can enjoy home cooking and still achieve your dreams. Unfortunately, he wasn't able to savor it.

Photograph by James A. Ewing.

"Ever After"

It has been said that beauty is in the eye of the beholder. This is especially true when it comes to one's hometown.

In recent years, Modesto has unfortunately and undeservedly been included in the top ten on a number of lists about places to live, work, or retire. Most haven't been flattering. These are lists compiled by people who don't live here. People who look at us through the prism of statistics and interviews with jaded refugees. Bloggers who sit at their computers and use Wikipedia for their facts and figures. News readers who get their information from less than reliable or objective sources. Few, if any, have ever set foot in our little town. Some are folks who grew up here, had a bad experience, left, and continue to blame their malaise and misfortune on the town. Regrettably, these people have not, do not, and will not look below the surface. Or spend time here. It's impossible to know a place without being a part of the fabric of that place.

Yes, we have homeless, but we have people and agencies that try to help them. We have crime, but we have a conscientious corps of vigilant law enforcement and charitable volunteers to counteract it. We have eyesores, but we have devoted community activists who work very hard to beautify and maintain our city. We have pollution, but we have committed citizens working diligently every day to reverse that. We have poverty, but we have organizations and schools, selfless advocates and educators dedicated to assisting people to change their circumstances. We have auto theft and meth labs, but we also have *Graffiti Summer* and farmers' markets. We are far from the urban cultural centers of San Francisco or Los Angeles, but we have a symphony orchestra, an opera company, a performing arts center, a theater company, a minor league baseball team, and a ballet company. For every Scott Peterson, there is a George Lucas, Jeremy Renner, or Ernest Gallo. A town is its people. And ours are stellar.

I have lived in many places. I have visited many more. Each has its pluses and minuses. It's unfair to paint an entire people and place with the same, broad brush. It's demeaning, insulting, and incorrect. Akin to viewing all Southerners as ignorant racists, young black men as heartless thugs, Californians as dreamy tree-huggers, or wealthy people as arrogant elitists.

Modesto has grown and changed, as everything does. It is no longer a town of 30,000, which is how big it was when I was growing up. People need to spend time here to get the whole picture, which CNN, *Forbes Magazine*, and the other media outlets that portray us poorly, do not do. A collection of photographs posted and promoted by CNN, which originally prompted this essay, are no different than the images shot in 1936 by Dorothea Lange during another tough economic period. Lange's images did not show the entire picture then and CNN's images do not show the entire picture now.

Short-attention-span, bite-size snapshots of a people or a place do more harm than good. I love my hometown. We have warts, but we also have unexpected beauty. Beauty is indeed in the eye of the beholder. So is blight. People will see what they want to see. You cannot paint it black, nor can you paint it white. It is, like all things, a spectrum of gray.

There are many in Modesto who are dedicated to making this a better place. Who are willing to praise it, not damn it. Join us. Do your part. Ever After is Here and Now. Make a difference by making it better.

"The Singularity"

Yesterday a child came out to wonder
Caught a dragonfly inside a jar
Fearful when the sky was full of thunder
And tearful at the falling of a star
– Joni Mitchell, "The Circle Game"

It's tough being the first to roll out of the womb. The oldest. *Numero uno*. Fortunately, and

unfortunately, you would always be the aborigine; the inaugural. The first to …

Start the Circle Game.
Be bragged about.
Have a birthday.
Crawl then walk.
Use the potty.
Get a tooth and lose a tooth.
Get spanked.
Believe in Santa, the Easter Bunny, and the Tooth Fairy.
Stop believing.
Go to school.
Skin a knee.
Ride a bike.
Watch Roy Rogers on TV.
Get a friend and lose a friend.
Get mad and get even.
Forgive and forget.
Get the measles, mumps, and croup.

Get well.
Throw a ball.
Catch a ball.
Break a window.
Fall down and get back up.
Get a job and lose a job.
Drive a car and crash a car.
Go to the prom.
Drink and smoke and do the hootchie-coo.
Fall in love.
Go to college.
Experiment.
Grow hair and lose hair.
Get married and divorced.

There are as many stereotypes about birth order as there are grains of sand in an hourglass. The oldest is smart, neat, and well-behaved. The middle child is sloppy. The youngest a ham.

I fit the profile. I was …

Dependable. You could count on me.
A high achiever. I loved the little gold stars.
A seeker of approval. I worked hard for the smiles.
A perfectionist. I dotted the i's and crossed the t's.
Selfish. I didn't like people messing with my stuff.
Determined. When there was a job to be done, I was the one to do it.
A leader. I was comfortable being in charge.
Organized. I preferred a place for everything and everything in its place.
Eager to please. I did the dance.
Non-confrontational. I avoided trouble at all costs.
A know-it-all. I liked being right.
Controlling. I didn't mind orchestrating things.
Protective. I got used to running interference.
Over-responsible. I sometimes took it too seriously.
Well-behaved. I took pride in being the good son.
Careful. I very seldom took chances.
Predictable. I was a lot like the seasons.
Concerned. I wanted everyone to be happy.
The glue. I liked putting people together and keeping them together.

If you were a firstborn, the following feelings were familiar. "Everyone depends on me." "I can't get away with anything." "I don't get to be a kid." "Why do I have to do it? Nobody else does anything around here." "Why should I act my age?" "How come I'm responsible for what my little brother or sister did?" "It wasn't my fault."

As the pioneer, you were the guinea pig. The test-tube baby. Your mom and dad got to make all the mistakes with you. A firstborn was naturally and realistically a sort of experiment for the new parents; a mixture of instinct and trial-and-error. I have a flat spot on my head because my mom allowed me to lie in one spot too long as an infant while my skull was forming. My folks were tougher on me when it came to behavior, grades, and expectations. But I was also their only priority, their only responsibility. It was worth it.

As the oldest, I would always be the only one in my family who would ever have my parents completely to myself. I lost that singularity, my seat on the familial throne, when number two arrived. As other brothers and sisters came along, they shared the load. But they paid very close attention to what I had done. They would almost always look to me for answers and perhaps guidance. Those expectations were weighty. Heavier than my brother. I hated to disappoint people. I wasn't perfect. I made mistakes. I vividly recall the time my youngest brother argued with a store clerk over the correct title of a record. The clerk was right. I was wrong. But my sib was going to defend me to the end because he was convinced I was always right.

Over the years, I did and have done a lot of stupid, selfish things to my brothers and sisters. It wasn't right and I knew it. I didn't mean to do it. It just seemed to happen. I felt badly about it, but I couldn't seem to help myself. I guess it was all part of growing up as the eldest. I was selfish and didn't always think things through. After I'd done whatever I'd done, I'd invariably wish I could take it back. It was always too late, and the damage had been done. I sometimes wondered what I would have been like and how different the world would have been if I had been anywhere else in the birth order.

But that's not the way it played out. I was the caretaker. Then. Now. And always.

However, there was one thing I wasn't the first to experience. And it took my little brother before his time.

My child arrived just the other day,
He came to the world in the usual way.
But there were planes to catch, and bills to pay.
He learned to walk while I was away.
And he was talking 'fore I knew it, and as he grew,
He'd say, 'I'm gonna be like you, dad.
You know I'm gonna be like you.'
– Harry Chapin, "Cat's in the Cradle"

"Stick Around"

Dandelion Wine by Ray Bradbury is a book about a boy a lot like me. In that novel, 12-year-old Douglas Spaulding says, "You can't depend on people because they go away. People you know fairly well die. Your own family dies. So, if trolleys and friends can go away forever, or fall apart or die, and if someone like Great-grandma, who was going to live forever, can die, if all this is true, then I, Douglas Spaulding, someday must die."

I guess I was thinking about that one Saturday afternoon in early May while my brothers and I were pulling weeds as part of our weekly chores. Well, I was pulling weeds. They were chasing ants and butterflies and grasshoppers.

I stopped hoeing and looked at them both. Tim finally noticed the quiet and turned around. Willy did, too.

"What?" Tim said.

"Look," I replied, "sometimes, uh, a lot of times, you guys bug me, and I don't like you. You're always following me and getting in my stuff and telling Mom or Dad about something that I did and not doing your chores, so I have to do them for you. Stuff like that, you know."

"Yeah, I know," they both said and giggled.

"So, even though you do all that and it makes me mad, I like having you around, okay."

"Sure, okay," Tim replied.

"So, don't go anywhere."

"Where we gonna go?" Willy asked.

"Just be careful, got it?"

"Got it," they both said again.

I went back to trying to control my little bit of the world, just as a dirt clod exploded at my feet.

Image by Galina Peshkova. ©123RF.com

"Snowflakes"

Met my old lover in the grocery store
The snow was falling Christmas Eve

It was foggy and cold. The streets damp. The streetlights muted. The multicolored bulbs muffled. It was Christmas in the Central Valley.

I was on holiday break. UC Davis was out for two weeks. It was time to close the books and catch up. I pulled up outside in the white '52 Chevy.

We hadn't seen each other for some time.

She was living in the top floor apartment of an old, converted house on the corner of Magnolia and Needham. It was a studio tucked beneath the steeply peaked roof. Cramped but comfortable. She had decorated it with concert and blacklight posters, God's eyes, hanging plants, tie-dyed tapestries, and some of her artwork. All the pop culture touchstones of winter 1969. The year everything changed.

I hadn't treated her right the last time we had been together. It was summer a year earlier. We had made love in her parents' backyard while they were traveling. I had left. I hadn't called her. I went back to school. It was a pattern with her and me.

I was surprised she agreed to see me when I called. But that was the way she was. Kind, generous, and forgiving.

We drank a toast to innocence
We drank a toast to now
We tried to reach beyond the emptiness
But neither one knew how

It was cold outside. Warm inside. The four, four-paned windows looking out on Magnolia were misted over. Perched on the wooden table in front of the two center windows was a small green Christmas tree dotted with home-made decorations and draped in plastic tinsel. Small snowflakes had been cut from white construction paper the way we had done them in elementary school. She had hung them with red ribbon from the top of the window frame.

We talked of her work. We talked of my studies. Both were going well enough. We talked of our families and friends. All were doing well enough. We talked of the world. All was not merry and bright.

She lit a small white candle and set it beside the tree. She put a Peter, Paul and Mary Christmas album on the stereo. She turned off the lights. We sat on the edge of her bed and passed the joint back and forth. We stared through stoned eyes at the swirling snowflakes. It felt like we were back in high school. It was comfortable. I felt like I could stay here forever. That we could stay together. That we could make a life. It was time to think about things like that. We were old enough. We made love. And I left. I didn't call. I went back to school. Again. The same old pattern.

She died young. I think of that night each Christmas and every time I pass the apartment house. I wish she were still here so we could talk about that time together. And the other times. So we could talk about what a fool I was. So I could apologize and perhaps recapture or relive a moment in time. They say regrets are a waste of time. But I regret not having the chance to tell her how much I loved her; how beautiful and amazing she was. How much I missed her. Perhaps if I had, perhaps if others had, she might still be with us.

This is one of many such memories about her and others conjured each time I listen to "Same Old Lang Syne" by Dan Fogelberg. This particular memory is one in a long line of regrets. Of missed moments. Of things allowed to slip by. Of not being in and savoring the moment. Of always looking ahead. At what's next. Of worrying about missing something. And not recognizing what was right in front of me.

I suppose as you get older, these regrets become more apparent, more pressing, more urgent, more painful. I will forever be sorry.

Just for a moment I was back at school
And felt that old familiar pain
And, as I turned to make my way back home
The snow turned into rain
– "Same Old Lang Syne" Dan Fogelberg

Photograph by Vanston Shaw.

"Nicknames"

In Loving Memory of Hoden, Jorge, the Dancing Bear, and Bo'Re.

My family loved nicknames. We gave them to each other, to relatives, to friends, even strangers. My dad was known as "Tooter," for his clarinet and saxophone playing in high school. My mom was known as "Dynamite," for being who she was. My oldest little brother Tom was "T-Honey" and "Bone Sights, Jr." My youngest little brother Wendell was "Spindle Fibers," "Harry Joe Brown," "Wee-Stoner," which was shortened to "Stoner" and took on different implications as he grew up and became a musician. My oldest little sister Deb was "Hey Do" or "Hey Dot" and "Debo." My youngest little sister Cindy was "Sammy," which is the name most people know her by still. My nicknames included "Whitey," "Pinky," "Ken Bob," as well as "Chink Eye" and "Kenji," which was homage to Japanese American, big-time wrestler, Kenji Shibuya, and my squinty eyes.

My college buddies were Gover, Wally Gator, the Red Herring, and the Mudcat.

My fellow "Mud Bowlers" took nicknaming to a whole different level. "The Mud Bowl" was a football game we played every Thanksgiving. The Davis High Class of '66 against the Downey High Class of '66, Davis Class of '64, and some younger brothers and friends. This same group of guys assembled every year at Thousand Oaks Park in Modesto for almost 50 years.

We all had nicknames, immortalized in the annual tribute video I created for the night-before-the-big-game banquet. An evening of eating, drinking, catching up, and trash talking.

In addition to Whitey and T Honey, there was Jorge, Si, Bo'Re, Goat, Hands, Scur, Vanston and Lanston, Kipling, Goat, Big Cou and Little Cou, Stein, Hollywood, Pancho, Big Boy, Dancing Bear, Roy Boy, Fast Johnnie, Hoden, Putz and Henniputz.

If we gave you a nickname, that meant you were accepted into the clan. I guess it was our way of controlling our world. If we could name it, we could claim it.

Image by scanrail. © 123RF.com.

"Comes a Time"

"Come on, dude," I said. "I <u>do</u> know you better than that. You never did anything in your life that didn't benefit you. What blows is, it always did. Nothing ever worked out for me. I mean I'm still here doing the same old shit. You've been a player. On the big stage."

"That can cut both ways," my friend replied.

"Bullshit. But, hey, I'll never know. I'll always be the guy telling the story, not the guy the story's about."

"And how do those stories always end?"

I didn't have an answer.

"Yep, they're a disaster."

"I feel for you, but I can't reach you."

"Sure you can."

My friend smiled that winning smile that made him big man on campus back when we were in high school.

"Screw you. It's true and you know it. Always in the right place at the right time. Always sliding through. Nothing ever sticks. A real Teflon man."

The smile on his face snapped off as the nightmare came flooding back.

"No hard feelings," he said

"No hard feelings. I'll send you a fan."

I thought as we sat there nursing our beers, *There's a moment in everyone's life when it's time to be the person the story is about instead of the person telling the story. Time to be the person they write about, not the person doing the writing. That time had come for me. Would I have the guts and confidence to grab the ring, or would I let it slide by?*

Only time would tell.

"Trinity"

The Joker. The Musician. The Cowboy. The wholly and unholy trinity.

I've been fortunate to have three people in my life who I could always talk with about sports, music, and beer. My best friend, George, known to some as Jorge, always the joker. My youngest brother, Wendell, better known as Stoner, the rock 'n roller. And my college buddy, Mike, AKA Wally Gator, forever the cowboy.

Any time I wanted to catch a game, listen to a song, or sip a cold one, I could count on at least one, and sometimes all three, to be right there with me.

Sadly, the legendary trio is no more. They're all gone. Much too young. Now, conversations about sports, music, and beer are mostly between me, myself, and I. There are a handful of stand-ins, but it's not the same.

I created a memorial video for each one. I pored over countless images and tried to select just the right songs to convey the essence of their lives, which, of course, involved sports, music, and beer. It was painful because I realized we wouldn't be making those memories anymore. When I finished Gator's tribute, who was the most recent to leave us, I swore it would be the last. It was just too damned hard. I said adios and happy trails to The Three Amigos.

Until we meet again.

"In My Life"

For when that day comes.

My favorite novel was *Dandelion Wine* by Ray Bradbury. One summer's day, the protagonist – 12-year-old Douglas Spaulding – reflects on mortality. On how friends leave, and family members die. He realizes that someday he, too, must die.

I read that book every year so I could savor the wonder and joy of life that Bradbury described. And it always made me think of the wonder and joy of my own life. And my mortality.

There are places I'll remember
All my life though some have changed
Some forever not for better
Some have gone and some remain
All these places have their moments
With lovers and friends I still can recall
Some are dead and some are living
In my life I've loved them all
Lennon & McCartney, "In My Life"

I was born in Lathrop, California, and raised in Modesto. I lived in Davis, San Francisco, Hayward, Montara, and Oakdale, California, as well as Honolulu, Hawaii. I spent most of my life in Modesto, the town where summer lasts longer. I attended nearly every elementary school in town as we

Baby Boomers moved through the school system, including Washington, Enslen, Beard, and Garrison. I moved on to Roosevelt and then Davis High. I received my A.A. at Modesto Junior College, my B.A. and Elementary Teaching Credential at UC Davis, and my M.A. at San Francisco State University.

I was a writer, producer, and director of informational, promotional, and entertainment media for some of the world's largest corporations, including Bechtel Corporation, Levi Strauss & Co., and the E.&J. Gallo Winery. I taught a mass communications and film appreciation class at Modesto Junior College. I also wrote short stories, novels, children's books, screenplays, nonfiction books, and stage plays, mostly about my hometown and the Central Valley.

I served on the board of directors of the State Theatre, produced a number of community events there, and helped launch the State Cinema Club. I helped found the Friends of George A. Rogers Neighborhood Park, which allowed friends and family of my good friend George to accomplish a wide variety of projects for the airport neighborhood. I also participated in a wide variety of activities to help make my hometown a better place to live and work, including Graffiti Summer, Valley Music Institute, the Amgen Tour, the McHenry Museum & Historical Society, PorchFest, the Graffiti USA Museum, and the Graffiti Cruise Route. I've helped raise money for and awareness of Grace M. Davis High School, the University of California, Davis, the Gallo Performing Arts Center, and the Prospect Theater Project. For over fifty years, I played in the annual Mud Bowl, a yearly rite that allowed all who participated to be kids again. I played Little League and Babe Ruth, then transitioned to intramural, city, SOS, and senior league and tournament softball nearly every Spring and Summer. I was a fan of the Niners, Giants, and Modesto Reds, now the Nuts. I looked forward to celebrating Thanksgiving, Christmas, and the 4th of July with family and friends. I appreciated the music made by family, friends, local musicians, and better-known acts like Buffalo Springfield and all its variations through the years, including Neil Young, Poco, Crosby, Stills, and Nash. And summer wouldn't have been summer without hearing at least one Everly Brothers' or Beach Boys' song.

In my life, I accepted that change was inevitable, expectations were unreal, loneliness was absolute, and laughter was essential.

I tried to make a difference in my world. I helped put people together and helped keep them together. A musician friend once dubbed me the "Town Crier." Another friend called me the "Pied Piper." I gave back to my community. I tried to be a good older brother to Tommy and Wendy and Debbie and Cindy, as well as a loving uncle to my nephews Jason, Trevor, and Jackson, my nieces Connie, Kathleen, and Lauren, and my grand-nephews Connor, Dashiell, and Bodhi and grand-niece Teagan. I tried to be a supportive, nurturing, and loving companion to my wife, Robin, and our children, Tyler and Eric, as well as a good father-in-law to Rebecca and grandfather to Cayetano. I hope I succeeded.

My favorite movie of all time was *It's a Wonderful Life*. Director Frank Capra showed us what the world would have been like if one man hadn't been born. An ordinary guy named George Bailey, who believed in human dignity, community, and family.

At the end of the movie, Clarence – his guardian angel – tells George: "Each man's life touches so many other lives. And when he isn't around, he leaves an awful hole."

When I'm gone, I hope – like George – I will be remembered.

And though you have forgotten
All of our rubbish dreams
I find myself searching
Through the ashes of our ruins
For the days when we smiled
And the hours that ran wild
With the magic of our eyes
And the silence of our words

And sometimes I wonder
Just for a while
Will you remember me
Tim Buckley, "Once I Was"

"On Being a Central Valley Writer"

This valley after the storms can be beautiful beyond the telling,
Though our city-folk scorn it, cursing heat in the summer and drabness
*   in winter,*
And flee it – Yosemite and the sea.
They seek splendor, who would touch them must stun them;
The nerve that is dying needs thunder to rouse it.

I in the vineyard, in green-time and dead-time, come to it dearly,
And take nature neither freaked nor amazing,
But the secret shining, the soft indeterminate wonder.
I watch it morning and noon, the unutterable sundowns;
And love as the leaf does the bough.

This poem was written by William Everson, the Beat Friar. Another Central Valley patriot. He loved this Valley. Many of us have lost our connection with it; with what made us who we are. In all its kaleidoscopic glory. The familiar sight of the sun low on the flat horizon. The soft sound of rustling grape vines. The cool touch of flowing rivers. The sweet taste of a fresh peach. The memory-etching smell of irrigated soil. Here in this part of the planet, we are all linked by the land and this place we call home.

"If we are fortunate, if the gods and muses are smiling, about every generation someone comes along to inspire the imagination for the journey each of us takes."
– Bill Moyers in conversation with Joseph Campbell, The Power of Myth

The life and writings of Joseph Campbell have inspired me from the moment I first read *The Hero with a Thousand Faces*. Like Campbell, I believe in the power and promise of the hero's journey and the stories that unite us all.

Today, life is chaotic, fragmented, and out of balance. Our body, mind, and soul are no longer in sync. As far back as we can remember, the shaman has been called upon to balance and align the temporal, intellectual, and spiritual worlds. The shaman journeyed to unknown places beyond time and space, endured ordeals and tests, and returned with messages of healing and enlightenment for the community.

The writer is the modern-day shaman. Like the ancient shaman, the writer descends into his own personal depths in order to return with a reward for others. And that is the purpose of writing. To find some universal message or experience in our selves about who we are and the world in which we live and share it with our community.

"All good stories are out there waiting to be told in a fresh, wild way. Life is like a recycling center, where all the concerns and dramas of humankind get recycled back and forth across the universe. What you have is your own sensibility, insider pathos or meaning."
– Anne Lamott, Novelist and Essayist. Bird by Bird

When I encounter broadcasters, columnists, or bloggers who talk or write about the "narrative" and "storyline" of a particular political party or candidate or the "brand message" of an individual, company, or organization, I realize that everyone is a storyteller, everyone has a story to tell, and everyone appreciates a story well-told. Our lives, our experiences, and our world view are our stories. And each of us tells our stories from that unique perspective, whether it's in a novel, a song, a painting, a poem, the volunteer work we do, or the way we live our lives.

Michelangelo believed that every block of marble already contained a statue, and it was the job of the sculptor to discover it. The same is true of the writer. We all carry the stories within us, we just need to find them and share them.

I have always loved stories and respected storytellers. Whether they are novelists, poets, playwrights, video game designers, screenwriters, corporate communicators, or stand-up comedians. All of these individuals are telling stories. This love for the written word probably started with my book report club in elementary school and my love of comic books and the animated movies of Walt Disney.

Over the years, I have attempted to do as much as possible related to telling stories. I have written novels, children's books, screenplays, a sitcom pilot, and a stage play. I have designed, written, and produced corporate sales and training programs, as well as interactive video games. I have written and produced radio and television commercials. I have written poems and songs, as well as articles for magazines and newspapers.

I am, have been, and always will be a storyteller.

The world is made up of stories, not atoms.
– Muriel Rukeyser, Poet

About the Author

Ken White retired from the worlds of advertising, corporate communications, and interactive entertainment to concentrate on writing and community service.

He received his A.A. degree at Modesto Junior College, his B.A. and teaching credential at UC Davis, and his M.A. at San Francisco State University. He has taught mass communications and film appreciation at Modesto Junior College.

Born in Lathrop and raised in Modesto, California, he continues to live in his hometown. He is married to Robin and has two adult stepsons, Tyler and Eric. He has written novels, screenplays, short stories, stage plays, childrens' and non-fiction books. Most of his stories are about his hometown and the Central Valley heartland.

www.facebook.com/ken.white.7106

Other Books by Ken White

Tyranny of the Downbeat

Sarah's Game

Getaway Day

Nights on the Point

That Happiness Thing: A Hometown Fable

Twelve Days of Central Valley Christmas

Touchstones: Life and Times of Modesto

Brighter Day

Counting on Christmas

'Twas the Night Before Christmas ... In Modesto

www.ingramcontent.com/pod-product-compliance
Lightning Source LLC
Chambersburg PA
CBHW081955210726
48294CB00014B/2004